Outlaw Kind of Love

Prairie Devils MC Romance

Nicole Snow

Content copyright © Nicole Snow. All rights reserved.
Published in the United States of America.
First published in February, 2014.

Disclaimer: The following ebook is a work of fiction. Any resemblance characters in this story may have to real people is only coincidental.

All individuals depicted in this work are adults over the age of eighteen years old.

Description

OUTLAW LOVE: RUTHLESS, POSSESSIVE, EXPLOSIVE…AND WORTH IT?

Rachel Hargrove's sheltered life comes to a screeching halt when an unthinkable family betrayal turns her over to a savage motorcycle gang. Just when it seems her nightmare fate is sealed, a beautiful savior appears, the Vice President of the rival Prairie Devils MC. With her new protectors, Rachel faces a whole new life she never could've imagined…

Jack "Throttle" Shields never wanted an old lady. One look at the beautiful angel cowering in his enemy's clutches changes all that. Starting a war with the Raging Skulls MC to haul Rachel onto his bike and into his bed is just the beginning.

When Jack stakes a claim, he goes all in. War with the Skulls and a sinister Mayor is just the price of making Rachel his, and only his. But love invites blood and tragedy in an outlaw's life.

Just when it's looking up for his MC and his new woman, a savage attack blows the lid off everything. Revenge possessed Jack makes Rachel take a hard look at how far she's willing to go to surrender her heart.

Will she weather an outlaw's storm, or will the nightmare return – this time for good?

Note: this is a dark and gritty MC romance with language, violence, and love scenes as hard and raw as they come. Forbidden love is never easy!

I: Backstabbing Bastard (Rachel)

I didn't understand why he was tearing up. It scared the hell out of me.

Dad never cried. One minute, we were having a perfectly normal conversation as I rode in his big shiny Escalade. We were talking about something or other, my intern plans in the Fall at the veterinarian's office, or maybe what he was going to get his new girlfriend for their six month anniversary.

For once, he wasn't berating me about putting college on hold or whining about the way I dressed. He was in a good mood, and happiness was rare for my father.

Then his face went dark. We pulled off the highway into an empty lot, an abandoned weighing station for big rigs that hadn't been torn up yet.

"Hey! What's up, Dad? Why are we stopping here?"

He shook his head. A slow, red faced shake, as if it took all his strength to turn the wheel, guiding the vehicle to the side of the road.

I looked out. A blinding orange summer sun was just setting over the distant ranches, sending us into an early North Dakota night.

"I'm…I'm so sorry, Rachel. If there were any other way to avoid this, I would. God, please forgive me."

My heartbeat doubled. And that was before I heard the terrible roar up the road, the deafening blast of motorcycle engines. *A lot* of motorcycles.

"Dad? Dad! What the fuck!"

His face tightened. "Stop using that language. I don't care how hard things are about to get. You'll keep acting like a lady…no matter what they do to you."

The last part croaked out under his breath. His face crinkled and lost a few of the tears pooling in his eyes. He wiped his wet cheeks as five or six hairy bikers encircled us, bringing their bikes to an abrupt stop.

They had us surrounded. Confusion and terror gave way to panic. I began to scream, pounding on the glass window and reaching for the handle.

Not that I could've outrun them. Big, powerful, and ruthless men like that?

Good luck. And all the luck in the world had abandoned me.

Fight-or-flight kicked in. Dad clicked the lock shut before I could pop the door, reluctantly lowering the window as a man who looked like a bearded gorilla appeared at his side.

"You got her or what?"

"Yeah. Don't hurt my Rachel. Please. I've given you everything you wanted and more."

The stranger tipped his head back and laughed. It was a bawdy, harsh sound, almost as fearsome as he looked. He reminded me of a pirate captain from those cheesy old movies, but there was nothing lighthearted about this.

"Mister Mayor, we're the ones doing your ass a favor. And don't you forget it."

Dad's face turned beet red. His head looked like a fat, wrinkled sac of gunpowder ready to go off.

"I won't forget," Dad said with a sigh.

I blinked. Jesus, what was this?

Nobody ever got away with talking to my father, the mighty politician, that way.

"Good man. Now let the bitch out. Tell her not to run. Wouldn't want Blow's hands to rough up that pretty little face."

I stopped pounding my thighs in panic. My arms, my legs, the very blood pumping through my veins went numb. I turned to Dad one last time, defeated and horrified.

"Do what he says, Rachel. This is…this is for the good of our family. You'll understand someday."

I didn't move. On the driver's side, he punched the button for the lock. I heard the click and then the door flew open.

One of those big hairy apes was on me, unbuckling my seat belt, dragging me out of the car. My throat was already hoarse from crying and screaming, but I had plenty more for them.

"Mmmm! Got a real wild one here, Venom. You want to ride with her or should I?"

My little wrists flailed backwards, slapping at him pathetically. Dad's Escalade chugged to life, and I watched him drive away, beating a retreat from the horror show he'd directed.

"Give her here!" The bigger, older man who'd been talking to Dad snarled, reached forward, and picked me up by the waist.

He threw me across his shoulder like a caveman. I beat on his back until my hands hurt.

No effect. The ogre didn't let up as he carried me several feet to his waiting bike, and parked me on the backseat.

"You gonna shut up or am I gonna have to make you? I'm not listening to this shit all the way to Fargo."

I ignored him, sobbing quietly in my seat. I couldn't make my limbs move anymore.

The four bikes up ahead thundered as the guys revved their engines. Venom threw his leg over the bike just in front of me, and told me to hold on tight.

This is fucking crazy! I'll go with you, asshole. But I'm not gonna touch you if it's the last thing I –

A resounding swipe to the side of my head silenced all my thoughts. He'd spun around and backhanded me. My whole body trembled in shock.

No man had ever hit me before. Let alone one who looked like an escaped con.

"When I talk to you, the answer is 'yes, sir,' or 'no, sir.' You give me the cold shoulder again and I'll rip it clean off, bitch. We're on a tight schedule. Got a quick meeting with some assholes and then it's a clean ride home to our clubhouse in Sioux Falls. You're Skulls property now."

He paused, lighting up a fat, reeking cigar. "Put your little hands around me and get fucking used to it. I'm not telling you again."

My brain locked up, scanning all its options. There was only one, and I did the sole terrible thing I could.

I obeyed.

Like a shaking animal, I leaned forward, grasping the demon's flabby body. Just then, I'd do anything to relieve the suffocating weight in my lungs, the agonizing certainty that this was bound to get a whole lot worse.

"Good girl," he puffed, blowing his stinking tobacco back in my face. "Let's ride."

I zoned out, somewhere between a waking sleep and a wide awake trauma. My hands stayed perched on his repulsive body, hovering near the place where his belt met his leather.

Venom shifted his hips occasionally. It didn't take a genius to realize he was fighting an erection.

When I noticed, I almost heaved, and it forced me deeper into my self-induced coma. I was alone with gnawing questions – almost as bad as the cold reality outside my head.

Why? Why, why, why had Dad given me over to these animals?

I knew he was into some shady shit. Shady was the middle name of our town, Cassandra, but he was the man who'd run on a platform of cleaning up the town, and never doing deals with the Prairie Devils MC like the last Mayor did.

Obviously, something horrible had changed his mind. He'd never been father of the year.

The Dad I knew was a cold, career driven man. Even holidays with him, the only times I really saw him, felt like carefully staged photo ops.

It only got worse after mother died. He hurled himself into politics, selling off the old family business, and dedicating his life to public service with a scary passion. He talked about it endlessly over those big family dinners, as if it was the most natural thing in the world.

I was only twelve when he revealed his grand plan to make me a Governor's daughter. First, the council seat, then the Mayor's office. With any luck, he'd get a state appointment or haul in some big cash from new friends, an easy bridge to North Dakota's lone Congressional seat and then the Governor's mansion.

When we were winding toward Fargo, I lifted my head, staring closely at my captor's back for the first time. I'd seen the Devils around town before – our little hamlet was home to their founding charter – but these guys didn't have the same winking devil and pitchfork patches I'd always known.

RAGING SKULLS MC, SIOUX FALLS was outlined in white banners on his leather in big blocky letters. The text patches surrounded a dark red screaming skull.

So much for those campaign promises, Dad. Looks like you've traded one group of crazy scum for another.

"What's so fucking funny?" Venom growled, his voice barely audible over the bike's roar and the nimble summer wind.

"Nothing," I muttered. I hadn't even realized I was laughing.

Jesus. My marbles were really rolling right out of my head, and he hadn't even made me touch him yet. Not like that.

I didn't want to think about it. To think that I'd saved my virginity for nineteen years, only to give it up to this beast, old enough to be my own father.

Like it or not, it was coming. I saw the way he looked at me when we stopped for fuel. Not to mention the sour, ratty little laughs of his henchmen.

"Hope you're well rested for a wild ride when we get home tonight, little girl," the man called Blow whispered into my ear when Venom was in the bathroom. "Our VP's gonna tear your sweet pussy up. Just hope there's still a little something left for the rest of us when he gets bored of you. The club needs new meat, and you're a very tasty looking cut."

I should've run then, should've screamed, should've done anything to flag down the attention of the old couple who ran that little gas station in the middle of nowhere.

Shoulda, coulda, woulda.

I knew all about the biker gangs, though. Our local Devils and the men who came through every year on their way to Sturgis protected their interests like hungry wolves.

Resisting would just get others killed, and I wasn't okay with that.

Back on the road, Venom took the lead, driving the short distance into Fargo. Soon, we were sloping into what looked like the entrance to a city park. The motorcycle's roar became more noticeable at the slower speed.

Several shadowy shapes on other bikes were waiting. More than just his guys.

"Keep your fucking mouth shut," he whispered behind me. "What goes down here is none of your business, and you're not gonna embarrass us in front of our new…partners."

The last word came after a pause, like he didn't want to acknowledge the group of strangers. Venom lifted himself off the bike, throwing my hands toward me in a flurry.

He walked behind me and grabbed the small bag in the little compartment. His men flanked him as he carried it forward in the darkness.

I couldn't see much of the other group in the dull orange light streaming down from the park's lone functioning lamp.

"Evening, guys. Got your shipment right here. Your toll for letting us through through Devil's territory, as promised." Venom's back was turned to me, but I knew he was smiling.

I'd seen his smile exactly twice. It was a big crooked grin with deep craters where several teeth were broken out.

Jesus. That's the smile you're going to see when he's got you under him, or somewhere even worse.

"Yeah, yeah," a new voice said. "Jonesy, get up here! Let's count this shit and make sure everything's here. You can never tell with these bastards."

The man came closer. I saw him in the faint light, a tall younger guy in his prime, maybe close to thirty.

He had a handsome face with medium sandy hair and long stubble. His bright eyes pierced straight through the pale orange fog. Broad shoulders, strong hips, the kind of man a girl would casually drool over if she was anywhere but here.

Venom's shoulders twitched. It was easy to see the stranger's bold defiance got underneath his skin. Mister Tall, Young, Dark, and Handsome had thrown disrespect in his face the same way that bastard had blown his cigar stink into mine.

A skinnier man ran forward, joining the young guy. They were both underneath the lights now, and I saw the trademark Prairie Devils patches on their leather jackets.

The two Devils began lifting big blocks in plastic bags out of the leather bag and counting. An older man with gray hair showed up behind them.

I'd seen him around town a couple times before. It was the President of the Devils, their founder, a man everybody called Voodoo.

"Hm. We're missing a couple, boys," skinny Jonesy said. "Want me to recount, Throttle?"

"No," the good looking guy said. "I counted right along with you, Jonesy. We're two short, Pop."

"What the hell is this?" Vodoo said. He turned away from Throttle – apparently his son – back to a very pissed looking Venom.

"That's the price of our last trip up near Canada for you assholes," Venom spat. "You wanted us to take that offbeat busted up road all the way to Montana…"

Venom stepped up, planting himself in the old man's face. "Well, one of my guy's got busted by a surprise border patrol pig about fifty miles from the border. Blew a couple tires on that shitty road too. You're lucky our whole fucking gun shipment didn't wind up in some sheriff's hands."

Throttle cut between the two men, his big fists coiled at his sides.

"I don't give a shit. You wanna do business going through Devils' territory, then you're gonna play by our rules." He raised one hand, planted it on Venom's chest, and gave him a shove.

Venom swung, but missed, and barely caught himself before crashing to the ground.

That claustrophobic ache in my chest was back. I couldn't breathe.

Jesus, if these guys are going to put me in the middle of a gang fight...I can't take it. I won't!

I broke down and started to cry. Loudly.

The rival gangs were circling each other beneath that jack-o-lantern glow, Raging Skulls and Prairie Devils ready to tear into each other like feral packs. My shrill sobbing seemed to give everybody pause in the stillness.

"Hold up, hold up. Let him get on his feet," Voodoo said. "It's not worth breaking the truce, son. Just as long as these fuckers go back across the border and cough up our two missing keys of coke, plus interest. And I want them by tomorrow night."

Venom glared, kept his hands up, holding his boys back. The men were still sizing each other up, one wrong move away from a fistfight. Or probably something a lot worse than a hand-to-hand brawl by the way some of them were fingering their pockets.

I lost it. My nerves were fried. The latest uneven sob I gave up to the night became a full on scream.

"Hey, what the fuck is this?" Throttle crossed right past the glaring Skulls and saw me for the first time.

We locked eyes. I watched his widen, and then narrow as he creased his brow, hatred filling every part of him.

"Fuck! They've got a girl back here, Pop." He came closer, closer, until he was just a couple feet away. "Doesn't look good."

He looked me over, saw the red mark on my face. It had started to swell since Venom backhanded me on the cheek.

"She's hurt!" He growled, turning back to the men behind him, before moving all the way over to me. "Come on, baby. Let's get you off that grungy excuse for a bike."

I whimpered as his strong arms wrapped around me. More commotion among the group, threats and curses. They didn't stop him from pulling me off Venom's motorcycle.

"What the hell do you think you're doing, Voodoo? This is our god damned business. Not yours." Venom tore himself away from the old President, staring at Throttle and I. My mysterious savior wasn't slowing down.

"Put her back right now, asshole! Right. Fucking. Now! I had to bust good balls to get my hands on that fresh meat. You take her away from me and I'll fuck up your whole crew."

"Pop?" Throttle yelled over the Skulls roaring their agreement. "Still wanna keep that truce? Two keys of coke behind schedule is bad, but dealing with despicable fucks who beat up little girls…"

His words disappeared into a savage growl. Voodoo and Throttle stared at each other across the angry men lined up between us.

"Oh, God," I sputtered, struggling for breath.

"Just breathe! Breathe, baby, and keep walking with me. None of these shitheads are gonna lay another finger on you. I promise."

I saw Voodoo look from side to side, glancing at his boys. Then he gave them a slow, solemn nod. I threw myself into Throttle's side, burying my face, right as someone threw the first punch.

The sounds around me were terrible. Men screamed and swore, scratching and clawing at each other.

Throttle jerked away from me once. I screamed, suddenly all alone.

My eyes opened just in time to see him pick up Blow and throw him across the parking lot.

"Let's go!" His hand was on mine again, forcing me to keep moving. "See that bike over there? That's mine. That's where we'll be home free. Just keep on going and don't look at anything else."

We went right past several guys on the ground rolling around. The metallic echoes on the ground were too sharp to be fists or belt buckles. Had to be knives, hammers, and brass knuckles slapping the concrete, sometimes making softer cracks when they impacted flesh instead.

A second later, he had me settled on the back of his bike, leaning close to whisper in my ear. "Stay here. I gotta finish this shit so we can take off."

"No, don't go!"

I yelled after him, but he was already running into the fray. It looked like the Devils had the upper hand. I hoped so, anyway.

Several skulls were retreating toward their bikes. I saw Venom's big outline being helped up by another man. They helped him slow walk to the infernal machine I'd been forced to ride on.

"Voodoo! Voodoo!" He sputtered, over and over, dark blood flying from his lips. "Your MC just signed its death warrant! We're gonna rip all you Devil sons of bitches a new —"

A gunshot rang out. I flinched.

Throttle had his pistol drawn, breathing heavily. He fired the bullet across Venom's head – probably intentional.

I doubted a man like that ever missed. Jonesy was at his side, cradling a wound.

In a summer second, everybody packing heat had their handguns out and pointed at each other. Voodoo stepped forward, crossing the invisible boundary between the gangs.

"Get the hell out of here before I change my mind about letting you go with your lives. Truce is dead in another hour. Stay the fuck out of Devils' territory."

The old President cleared his throat and spat, barely missing Venom's boot. I could feel the hatred between them, crawling beneath the white hot tension thickening the summer air.

"Come on. We'll be back to settle scores later. We'll have sharper teeth too…"

The Devils didn't move until their rivals roared out of the parking lot. Several men grabbed the injured Jonesy and fished a first aid kit from one of the bikes.

It was like being tossed into a battlefield. My stomach churned.

I tried to ignore the screams as his biker brothers applied pressure to the cut in his side.

A strong hand squeezed my shoulder. I looked up at Throttle's face, firm but friendly, staring into those deep blue eyes.

"See? I said you were gonna be alright. My word in this club goes, second only to Pop's." He straightened his jacket, giving me a good look at the V. PRESIDENT patch on his left breast.

Father and son, thick as thieves. Even this crazy biker family isn't as fucked up as mine...

I should've done a better job controlling my thoughts. I started crying again, and then all over Throttle when he pulled me close, cradling me in his thick arms.

"Shhh. Don't say a word, baby girl. We'll sort all this shit out after we get you home."

Home.

I didn't have one now. That made me cry even harder, but his gentle touch kept it in check, prevented my sadness from turning into a full hissing, screaming lunatic fit.

We'll sort all this out. His words echoed in my head. *Guess we'll see about that.*

Throttle held me until my sobs lessened. He slipped onto the bike ahead of me, helping curl my hands around him. I instantly noticed a huge contrast with Venom's flabby belly.

The Devils' VP was way more fit than the ugly ogre he'd run off. Throttle looked like the very icon of what a knight on this steel horse should be.

"You good to ride, Jonesy?" He shouted.

I looked up and the skinny man nodded. "I'll manage. This run's only a little under an hour. Frannie can patch me up at the clubhouse."

"Hear that, boys?" Voodoo yelled over the roar of multiple bikes. "That's our cue to get ourselves out of this sorry shithole."

"Thanks for helping me, Throttle," I whispered just before we got on the road, my first real words to my savior.

"Anytime. And call me Jack. That's my real name." He reached down with one hand and patted mine. "Never got yours, baby girl."

"It's Rachel."

"Rachel. Rach. I like that."

Even after all the horror, the smooth way he said it made me smile.

II: Licking Everybody's Wounds (Jack)

Saving that angel took a lot out of me.

We sat around the big club table, unwinding with beer and whisky. I wasn't the only one who looked thoroughly whipped.

Pop was at the head, the gavel at his side. He sat up straight, but I knew his bad back was killing him.

He can't keep this shit up much longer, damn it. Makes me wish I'd given that bastard in Fargo more than just a warning shot. Would've saved myself some trouble down the line when I get the reigns.

"What's the story on the stowaway?" Creeper smiled at me across the table, his eyes totally hidden in the extra large shades he insisted on wearing in all but the darkest places.

"Quit calling her that, man," I said. "Dunno yet. Frannie's cleaning her up and getting some food in her belly."

"She'll live," Warlock said. "My old lady fixes folks right. You guys should see the patch up job she did on Jonesy."

"She's in good hands," I agreed. I turned to Pop. "Now that we've declared war on the Raging fucking Skulls, shouldn't we make sure our equipment's in order? We need an attack plan."

Pop narrowed his eyes. He did the right thing helping with the rescue and putting those assholes on the run. But he did it reluctantly, and I knew he blamed me for things going sour.

"We're gonna dig in and look alive. If there's one thing I learned in Nam, it's to keep on the defensive."

"What about a good offense being a fucking awesome defense?" Bolt slammed his whisky shot and clinked his glass on the table so hard it almost broke.

"He's right, Pop. Why not hit those assholes hard before they call in reinforcements from the south? Sitting here isn't gonna do us any good while they're planning the attack."

"You've got a lot to learn, son," he growled back, revealing none of the pain shooting up as his spine as he sat up straighter. "Before all you hotheads in the room go charging forward, take a second and remember what happened in Sturgis."

Everybody in the room cringed.

It happened just last year. Our charter was part of the honor guard for all the big groups flowing into the annual motorcycle rally. Along our route, we had everything from rowdy riding clubs to the most vicious one-percenter MCs under our wing.

Something was bound to go wrong. Sure enough, it did.

The Ontario Snakes, our old Canadian trading partners, got into it with the Grizzles from out West. I was riding with the Snakes on the road, trying to keep the two from tearing each other apart.

A Grizzly Prospect decided to swing his dick by running the Ontario Snakes VP off the road. Too bad that accident killed him, and then all hell broke lose.

Our MC stuck by the Snakes, our old allies. It was the right decision to keep our drugs and guns flowing across the northern border, but we let our buds take too much into their own hands to deal out vengeance.

We rode with them right into a Grizzly trap. Got both our Prospects killed and a whole lot of Snakes bit it too before the Grizzlies roared back to Montana licking their wounds.

I gritted my teeth. Nothing was worse than Pop being right. Nothing.

"Don't break your jaw, Throttle." Warlock smiled at me. "Your old man's right. We can't risk another dust up like that. More Feds are sweeping the Dakotas since the local police are in MC pockets half the time. You know what those RICO laws can do. Any big blowouts could fuck over our whole business if it attracts the wrong attention."

I didn't say anything. Warlock lived up to his name, a big man with bushy hair and a sick power to read faces. He was also our club diplomat and Sergeant at Arms, keeping our boys away from each other's throats and our associates too.

"I'm calling a vote," Pop said. "Let's get this shit out of the way so everybody's on the same page. All in favor of going on the offense against the Raging Skulls, speak up now. We'll go with the Nays first."

I stared at the table as he went around to the seven of us. Jonesy got a proxy vote while he was laid up.

Everyone was a Nay. I saw it in their eyes before they spoke their vote aloud.

Even Bolt voted 'nay.' He always voted the same way as his cousins Shady and Pounce. Didn't matter if he felt differently.

None of my brothers looked me right in the eyes during the vote. They didn't like disappointing me, or else they were afraid I'd remember one day when I finally took over the club.

"Now the 'ayes,'" Pop said, fixing his harsh stare on me.

Why the fuck did he bother? I raised my hand and loudly confirmed my vote anyway.

But Pop's reason ruled the day. Unanimous except for my 'aye' vote. And that stunk like hell.

"It's a 'no go.'" Voodoo slammed down the gavel. "If nobody else has any business, then let's lighten up and get our shit in order. It's been a damned long day."

"Sounds good to me, Prez." Bolt lead everybody out, heading straight for the bar to wet his whistle with more brain blasting poison.

The door clicked shut behind Warlock, last out.

Pop and I were alone. I looked up at him, holding in my fury.

"You didn't have to humiliate me like that. Are you trying to make me look like a reckless asshole to the whole club?"

"Yeah, matter of fact I am, son. That's because you're acting like one."

If he wasn't my old man, I would've popped out of my chair and nailed him in the face. I dug my fists into my sides beneath the table.

"I did the only thing I could! Fuck, I saved us from a lot of trouble with those fucking jackoffs. Rachel can't be a day over twenty and she looked like a scared puppy. We don't need to be doing business with the Skulls when they're buying little girls."

"Rachel? That's the name of this bitch we have to go to war for?" Pop glared at me, shaking his head. "Shorting us on coke is bad. But trading bitches – if that's what was happening – is none of our business."

The holier-than-thou tone in his voice was really pissing me off. The older Pop got, the more righteous he sounded, and the less he really cared about much of anything.

It was a stupid fucking paradox. One that worried me too.

I bolted out of the chair and slammed my hands on the table in front of him, leaning into his face.

"This isn't you, Pop. This isn't our club. What the fuck happened to you? If you're really that tired of all this shit, then you ought to hang up your jacket and give the gavel to somebody with vision."

He reared up like he was about to punch me. Hesitated at the last second. Typical Pop – all bark, no bite.

It bothered me more that everybody else was starting to realize that too, brothers and enemies alike.

"Vision? That's what's gotten a lot of good men killed over the years, son. Took me half my life to figure that out. Club business *is* business, Jack, and there's no room for chivalry in blood and money."

My nostrils flared. A brutal heat throbbed through me, even as I held my gaze, staring into the eyes of someone I used to respect.

I tore myself away, walking past him, straight for the door. The big club banner with the pitchfork on it rippled on the wall with my movement, my burning need to get the hell out of here.

"Son, wait…" he called after me, weaker and softer than before.

"No." I ripped the door open and stopped. "Fuck you and your business. And if that's what this club's all about from now on, then fuck it too."

I slammed the door so hard the whole building shook. Several guys at the bar perked up at the noise, roused from their drunken stupor.

"She settling in okay?" I looked at Frannie, trying to ignore the killer rage dredged up by seeing Rachel with an ice pack tight to her pretty face.

"I think she'll make it, hon. I'd tell you it's a sure thing if I had a clean kitchen and infirmary to come to at the clubhouse…"

"Yeah, sorry about that. Prospects haven't been doing their job with all the excitement around here. Gonna have to have a heart-to-heart with them about all that."

Frannie's kind sass brought a smile to my face, despite all the bullshit. Warlock landed himself one hell of an old lady, the kind of girl who just got better with age, even if her looks didn't hold up the best.

Easy for you to say, a voice said in the back of my mind. *Let's see how well you look when you're pushing fifty.*

"I'd like that. But only if you guys wanna eat on time and get your wounds licked without an infection," Frannie said. "If it's not too much trouble."

"What Frannie wants, Frannie gets." I echoed the line the whole club used all the time, and that made her laugh.

"How 'bout you, baby girl?" I turned to Rachel. "Can you talk?"

She slowly drew the ice pack off her face. The swelling along her cheek looked redder than before, but going down. Good.

"Yeah. I appreciate everything…the rescue and the help here, I mean."

"Where'd you come from? Is there anybody we should call to help you out?"

Wrong question. Rachel stared down at her dusty shoes, fighting back a whimper.

Shit. I just wanted to get some information. Don't want to make this angel's tough time rougher.

"Jack! This isn't the best time to interrogate the poor girl. Get out of my infirmary if you're gonna do that. This is a place for healing." Frannie wagged her finger at me like an old mother.

She'd been a nurse before Warlock claimed her and moved her into the club full time. Good thing for the club that her sweet, but firm bedside manner didn't go when she quit her real job.

"No, it's okay," Rachel sniffed. "I...I don't know where to begin."

"Just tell me what happened," I said gently, moving close to her. "We're here to help you out."

I took her hand. Frannie eyed us with a skeptical wrinkle on her face, one beat away from swatting me away with the stethoscope around her neck.

"It was my father. He's the Mayor here, just elected...he drove me out to meet those other bikers. There was no warning. He just told me to get out the car and go with them. It was like he was giving up a stray dog!"

"Fuck," I muttered under my breath. I increased my hold on her precious hand, doing my best to soothe her worries away.

How the hell can anyone wipe away something like this? Had a feeling the new boss was a bastard.

I'd heard about Hargrove's election. Pop wasn't happy about it either. Hargrove had always been a pompous little man who stuck out like a sore cock in Cassandra.

He did business and politicking different than everybody else in this little town, but it had obviously won him enough friends in high places to win the election.

"It's gonna be okay," I told her. I was dead serious. "Why the fuck would he give you away to the Skulls? Did he say anything?"

She looked up, meeting my eyes. Soft starlight flickered through them as she struggled to remember the painful details.

"No, but the Skulls talked to him like he was their..."

"Their bitch?"

"Yeah." Sadness and anger seethed in her, making her pale skin flush. "Said it was for the good of our family."

"Shit. Those boys must have something on your old man." My face hardened. Just thinking about that puke Mayor made me want to pound on the nearest brick wall. "That doesn't excuse what he did to you. What kind of sick fuck won't fight for his own daughter?"

"He never cared about me." She shrugged. "I just never thought he'd do something like this."

"Well, he can't hurt you anymore, baby girl. You have my word."

It was hell holding back from touching her more. I wanted to bring her soft hand to my face, rub it gently across my stubble, then kiss it until I stopped all her tears cold.

What I wouldn't give to have Frannie in the other room.

"Listen to him, Rachel." Warlock's old lady piped up, laying her hand on my shoulder.

Pretty strong for an old lady, but I guess years of fixing broken bodies will do that.

"Thank you so much. Nobody's ever given me this kind of attention…you're better than my own family." As soon as the words were out of her mouth, she cracked.

I leaned into her, pulling her toward my chest. The shattered dove wept all over me and I let her.

Cry it all out. I'm gonna make Mayor Fuck-face pay a hundred times over, and the Raging Skulls too.

"Make sure she gets something good to eat, Frannie." The old lady raised a warning eyebrow at me. "Didn't mean it like that. Anything that comes out of your kitchen is fucking awesome, and you know it. I'll get on those newbies and whip 'em with my belt if I have to. If anybody around here needs clean facilities, it's you."

"You do that, Jack Shields."

I started to let go, but Rachel grabbed onto the leather jacket around my shoulders, hugging me closer. Frannie turned back to sanitizing some medical gear in the corner of our little makeshift sick room.

Warlock's old lady didn't see how one hand crept to the small of my girl's back. I pressed it there. If we were in one of those sappy supernatural shows, I would've transferred some strength into her.

"Stay strong, little Rach. You're gonna settle in here and be just fine. If there's nowhere else for you to go, then you can stay here as long as you'd like."

She answered by pushing her chin into my shoulder and sighing softly. Her breath wandered onto my neck, warm and sweet.

Rachel let go just in time for Frannie to turn around. Good thing too. I was getting harder by the second.

Inappropriate as all hell, but I couldn't help it. I turned, hiding my erection, annoyed with my body's natural response to that beautiful girl's touch.

I gave them both a quick wave goodbye and headed for the door.

I shut the door and walked down the hall to my room. Went right past the Purple Room on the way, where a couple of the club whores were spread out sleeping on plush burgundy.

I hesitated for a second. It had been months since I went to Rita and Michelle to blow off steam, and today I really needed it.

No. Keep moving.

Yeah, I could've barged in there and taken a girl to my room. Truth is, I didn't like fucking the whores much. I only used them when that pressure in my nuts became an ache that distracted me from everything else.

Didn't happen much. I usually had a real girl, the kind I liked to play up at the bars in every little biker hole from Cassandra to Chicago. They fell easy and often. I drove my dick hard and deep in their innocent little bodies, sometimes more than once, giving them the rough fantasy they all craved.

It came easy because they were exactly what I wanted: women outside club life. Pure, sweet, and corruptible, they offered me a touch I couldn't get from the whores, a little slice of the wide strange world outside MC life. The only life I'd ever known.

Some sweet merciful gods had given me a body women wanted since I bulked up like a man, and years in the club had hardened it to perfection. I should've been out fucking every night.

But casual hookups got old the older I got.

I'd never admit it to my brothers, let alone a hookup, but I was ready for something else. Pop wouldn't be around forever. His marriage with my junkie mom didn't last long, and he never went steady after that.

When he was retired and dead, I'd be the last Shields on earth. Not unless I found an old lady to claim, a beautiful baby girl to make lots of babies early and often.

Something about the idea of breeding like a tiger with the right mate turned my cock to steel. I stretched out on my old bed, patting the lump in my jeans with one hand.

Patience. Soon as this shit with the Skulls clears up, I'm gonna beat all these little personal demons cold.

I closed my eyes and tried to sleep. It wasn't easy with adrenaline and desire jacking up my blood, especially when I saw Rachel's tight young body every time my eyes twitched.

III: Rabbit in a Wolves' Den (Rachel)

I don't know how the hell I went to sleep that night, but I did.

Frannie's T.L.C. helped me more than I could've imagined. So did Jack's touch. The way he whispered to me and held me close took me far away.

In his arms, hell didn't burn so hot anymore.

I almost forgot about Dad's betrayal, and that messy ride with the Skulls. Almost.

I slept long and hard, way past noon. Remembering everything hit me in an awful rush.

Jesus. It's not a nightmare after all. What the fuck am I gonna do now?

Taking the pillows close to my face, I tried to blunt my crying and screaming, but of course I fell flat on my face.

Frannie was in the room across the hall, and she heard everything.

Next thing I knew, there was this big, kind lump sitting next to me, slowly stroking me back to sanity like I was her own flesh and blood.

"There there, young lady. Everything's gonna be alright. We won't let it be anything else when you've had two of the most powerful people in the club tell you you're gonna be okay."

Her joke brought a ghostly smile to my face. I sat up, leaned into her, trying to get my head straight.

"I don't know what the hell I'm doing. I have nowhere to go." I shook my head, already exasperated with being a nomad. "Half my friends are getting ready for college...they can't take me in. Extended family lives far away. And God! If anyone found out what Dad did...what if he sent them after me again?"

I wasn't certain what turned my stomach more; thinking about those greasy Skulls or my own father?

"Nobody's coming after you. I told you once and I'll tell you again: we won't let 'em. I'll keep telling you too, Rach, as many times as it takes to drill it into your pretty head."

There wasn't a shred of doubt in Frannie's voice. My body wanted to lay down on the bed and sleep the other twelve hours of the new day away. Good thing the saner part of me wouldn't allow that.

"Put me to work," I muttered.

"What?"

"Give me something to do around here. It's the least I can do with no way to pay rent." I watched her make a face like I was saying something totally crazy. "I really need a distraction too."

The lines in Frannie's face smoothed. She smiled, understanding at last.

"Come on. I'll let you get all cleaned up and start you something easy and mindless. Somebody will probably give me hell about having you doing Prospects' work, but I don't care."

Frannie didn't catch hell after all. By the end of the week, my hands ached from polishing floors and organizing cabinets. I felt like I'd just been through the gauntlet in a big kitchen and a hospital backroom.

In a way, it was refreshing to do real labor. Dad always protected me from that, having an underpaid cleaning lady on hand at all times.

Work burned away the pain. And burning off all that evil energy made me the most peaceful I'd been since arriving at the Devils' clubhouse.

Moving my body smothered fires in my brain. I didn't have time to cry when I threw myself into scrubbing, sweeping, and organizing. I worked until I slept easy – or easy enough – each night.

Didn't have time to let stupid little fantasies about my savior Jack go crazy either. But my daydreams still came in spurts, as unsettling as they were beautiful.

He'd been away for several days on club business – something about picking up supplies from another charter in International Falls – and a big part of me was glad.

If Jack had been here, I might've shunned work in favor of a very different, far riskier distraction.

The Skulls and my asshole father did more than nearly steal my virginity. They made me *fear* losing it to the wrong man.

After nineteen years, I'd held out for Mister Right, going on a few awkward dates with boys from school. They were too boring to make anything last, and rewarding these skinny dullards with sex was the last thing on my brain.

I pushed sex in the background altogether. I'd built it up to be this perfect, unachievable wonder. And to think it might be thrust on me at any time, against my will…

My capture, rescue, and arrival at the club had rebooted my brain. That filthy creep Venom had almost had his chance to wreck me for life.

I thought about sex a lot, and that just made me work harder. When I got into the rhythm of my chores, I could push it out of mind, including that sweet, handsome man who delivered goosebumps just by standing next to me.

Hard work saved me from myself, and from Jack. Even when I heard the guys taking the whores in that room down the hall, moaning and grunting out their pleasure, I ignored it with labor, anything to take my mind off dangerous temptations.

I'd even made a few friends. Tank and Freak, the club's two Prospects, both gave me massive props for cleaning up the Devils' messes better than they ever could.

At least I'm a natural at something Dad wouldn't approve of.

Actually, all the guys treated me like a polite guest, giving me way more credit than I would've ever given to these big fearsome bikers in my old life. Surprisingly, none of them tried to hit on me either.

Warlock was the only one around with an old lady. The rest of the guys were old or divorced or just throwing themselves at the two whores. I wondered what the hell made the Prairie Devils so different.

These guys were rough around the edges, but they didn't make my skin crawl like being around the Raging Skulls did.

Everything would've been awesome if it was just the Devils and Frannie I was dealing with. But then there were the whores.

The two women slunk around like cats when they weren't in that huge room decked with pink and purple.

The room creeped me out. It was like something a High School play would piece together to represent a Sultan's bedchamber.

The whores watched me working from a distance when they weren't in there fucking or sleeping. They never returned my smiles.

I was all ready to avoid those stone cold bitches on the evening Rita came up to me.

The skinny floozy was around thirty, wearing a tank top that revealed even more than her ass length skirt. I was cleaning the frames on the old photos in the hall when she appeared.

I stopped to look at an old picture of Voodoo, amazed at how much he resembled Jack in his younger days. The old man had been cagey to me since I arrived, but he looked downright handsome in his green fatigues, grinning at the camera with a fat joint in one hand and a rifle in the other.

"Hey, Princess. Whatcha doin'?" The sickly sweet and sour voice caught me by surprise.

I looked up as a set of long nails tapped hard on the glass of another dusty photo next to me. I knew it was Rita by that dark wavy hair with the purple skunk stripe down the middle. The other whore, Michelle, was bright blonde.

Her over-painted face leered at me with a big stupid smile. She clicked her jaw, chewing that potent grape bubble gum I always smelled wherever she'd been. It followed her like perfume.

"What does it look like? Cleaning up this place. That's how I earn my keep around here." I couldn't hide my irritation.

What the hell do you really want, anyway? I thought.

"Oh, so you think you're staying for the long haul?"

Pop!

Rita's big purple bubble exploded just inches from my face, flapping back into her mouth with a good tongue swipe. I wanted to punch her.

"Why wouldn't I?" I shrugged. "I kinda like it here."

"It's okay, girl. No need to get defensive. You've got all the guys and the only old lady that counts taking a shine to you. I can live with that."

"I hope so."

"Don't get any bright ideas about Jack. I don't like the way he looks at you for a guy who's got a good decade on you. Don't let him get liquored up and drag you back to his bed."

What the hell is this? A whore handing out advice about who I should sleep with?

I almost laughed at the irony. But Rita was really pissing me off, especially the steady *chomp-chomp-chomp* of those over-polished teeth.

"Care to tell me why that's any of your fucking business, and not my own?"

The waxy smile on her face melted. She stepped closer, shoving her big fake tits against mine. One accusatory finger shot out, its wicked nail pointed at my eye.

"Look, Michelle and I don't need another girl around here. Neither does the club. I get the fact that you're some little stray the guys picked up and want to nurse back to health like a wounded bird. If you want to stay, then you'd better learn your place. I don't like the way you're stepping outside of your cage, little birdie."

"Sounds to me like you're pissed because Jack won't fuck you as much as the other guys. Guess he prefers a different kind of woman."

Seething, I shook my hips for added emphasis. I lit a short fuse, and I knew it.

Rita flew forward, tackling me to the wall. She got a grip on one bicep and smashed her talon-like fingernails into me. I groaned, trying to shake her off, but she was taller and heavier.

"Listen to me, you nasty little bitch. You're too fucking stupid to know what's good for you. Michelle twisted my arm into telling you to back the fuck off the nice way. Now, we're going to do things *my* way."

Her nails scratched deeper at my skin. I squealed.

The panic was back, the same claustrophobic adrenaline rush I had on Venom's bike. Except this time, it wasn't staying contained. Not against another girl.

A terrible energy welled up in my stomach and exploded. I lunged forward, throwing everything my motion, grabbing at her right boob.

I caught her nipple and squeezed. Twisted.

Shocked, Rita fell back and screamed, an uneven catcall that echoed down the lonesome hallway.

Success. I'd broken her grip, and now I ran past her, but she caught my collar by the scruff of the neck and hauled me to her.

I kicked at her shins. Slurring her curses, the bitch went down, tumbling against the wall I'd been working on and almost demolishing several photos in the process.

Good! I hope she screws up something. Voodoo will chew her ass out for fucking up his precious memories...

"Get the fuck away from me!" She shouted. "You're a crazy little orphan shit, aren't you? Okay, I get it. I'll leave your wildcat crazy alone just this once. But you better listen to what I said, girl, or you'll wish the Skulls had you down on a dirty mattress raping your ass."

It took everything I had to keep my feet planted on the ground. It wasn't just the bitch fight. It was everything that had happened the past week welling up inside me, a powder keg going up in fire.

I doused them just in time. Rita flashed her hateful eyes at me one more time before turning smartly and walking back to her room. For the first time, the door to the whores' Purple Room slammed shut.

Still breathing heavy, I returned to work, studying the frames for any damage. No such luck.

Damn it. Guess I'll have to watch my back another way.

I brushed the whore's words off and tried not to think about them. But one thing kept nagging.

Is it really that obvious? This attraction to Jack?

I shook my head, muttering to myself. What little I knew about my savior told me those bitches wouldn't stand a chance of ever becoming his old lady.

Why, then, did they feel so fucking threatened?

A stupid crush like mine shouldn't keep them from banging their heads against the wall trying to get somewhere with him besides his bed. I was the one with the silly crush.

Not him.

It couldn't possibly be a two way street, could it?

I lifted the fifth heaping pack of thawed ribs onto the steel kitchen counter and sliced open the plastic. Frannie and I had a small army to feed, almost thirty hungry men between the club and its associates.

I wiped my brow. Who knew slamming cold meat around could be so damned exhausting?

"I'm glad your here, hon. Many hands make light work. Yours are a lot more nimble than Tank or Freak's too." Frannie smiled at me as she applied more barbecue sauce to our little production line.

"What's the occasion?"

She stopped in mid-spoon. "Haven't you heard? Jack's back. Got himself a hell of a good deal with the allied club up in Canada. That means more supplies and someone else putting the sting in the Skulls in Minnesota and Michigan for awhile."

My heart started to pound. Jesus, it had only been a solid week, but it felt like he'd been away forever.

"Will we get to join the festivities? Or is this for the boys only?" I asked sheepishly, checking the timer for the ribs still in the oven.

"You kidding? Some of the older guys will have their kids here tonight. The club's a family friendly place when it wants to be. I'm sure as hell going to be there when we're done with all this cooking. So are you."

Her look said she wouldn't tolerate anything else. That made me grin. It had been so long since somebody *really* wanted me around.

Me, Rachel Hargrove, attending a gathering for fun. Not because it was my duty as a politico's daughter.

The rest of the cooking went smooth. The Prospects helped us haul out the finished buffet to a huge table at the end of the bar.

I'd never smelled so much meat in my life. It was totally different from the square diet of greens and whole grains Dad always forced on me. He always said he didn't want me getting fat, but what he really meant is that he didn't want me eating anyway different from him.

My stomach growled during a break in the silence. Freak turned around and smiled.

"Jesus, Rach. Have a taste test. We got all the major food groups here: meatballs, ribs, wings, corn on the cob, and chips. Guess you'll have to wait a few more years for the whiskey one, though."

I couldn't help but smile back. Freak was almost as new as I was, a tall and heavily tattooed twenty-something year old guy. He was just a couple weeks into club life, bumped up to Prospect after being a hang around for about a year.

Not my type, but nice enough anyway. I took him up on his suggestion and loaded some meatballs onto my small plate. Frannie did too.

"Yep, we did the job right," she said in between bites. "About time too. I'm half-starved."

Everybody began streaming in about half an hour later. It was a strange carnival of big hairy men playing darts with their kids, arm wrestling for their turn at the bar's jukebox, in between stuffing their faces with beer and meat and then snoozing on the tables.

I fed myself and kept my distance. Watching Jack from afar kept me from falling asleep after all that work. For once, I didn't want it to lay me out too soon.

I wanted to go over and congratulate him. But fat chance of squeezing my way through the constant ring of boisterous brothers around him.

I think every man in that bar must've went by him at some point. Everybody except Voodoo, that is, who's absence was very obvious.

Didn't take a relationship counselor to know something was up between Jack and his old man. I only hoped it wouldn't weaken the club or lead to further drama. My arrival had already caused plenty.

"What's going on, girl? Why don't you get out there and join the games?" Frannie took my hand, stopping me when I tried to walk by her. "Half the guys are drunk off their asses. You could beat 'em all right now if you wanted to. There's even a little pot of play money on the line!"

"Thanks. Maybe some other time. I'm really feeling all that cooking in my bones."

She frowned, wrinkles showing in her forehead.

"You really want to spend some time with Jack, don't you?"

I started to sweat. Jesus, that sly smile on her face told me she knew everything.

"I...I just wanted to thank him. Can't imagine where I'd be if he hadn't pulled me away from the other MC." Actually, I could imagine it, and that made me want to thank him even more. "At least everyone else appreciates him around here too."

"You know, I've been meaning to pat him on the back myself. Let's go tell him in person. Come on." She stood and stepped forward, leading me on by the hand.

Frannie wasn't going to let me say no. Part of me thanked her persistence, and the other half coiled into an immature girl scared to death of coming face to face with the man she was crushing on.

We were halfway through the crowd when Frannie came to a dead stop.

"Wait, wait, wait. Maybe we should do this later, Rachel. He's got a lot going on right now…" The weird edge in her voice caught me by surprise.

Huh? Why the sudden change of heart?

I forced myself through the tight space between her and a big guy at the nearest table. Jack sat at the bar, completely surrounded by laughing bikers. He had the blonde whore on his lap, that slut they called Michelle.

She looked up from cooing in his ear and saw me. Her tongue poked out her gaudy red lips, teasing his earlobe.

Jack leaned back in rapture. His eyes opened, and he wore a shit-eating smile when his head rolled in my direction.

Time seemed to stop. Sound disappeared. His eyes went wide, swallowing me whole.

My heart pounded. The look on Jack's face switched from bliss to revulsion. A second later, Michelle looked pissed and disgusted as all hell as he stuck out his big hands, pawing her off him.

"Rachel! Rach, hey, wait. I need to talk to you…" I heard him say, his words faint and distorted over all the noise.

I wasn't doing anything consciously anymore. My feet turned, leading me back through the crowd, straight to a frustrated looking Frannie.

Breaking through the crowd, I knew he was coming after me, so I moved that much faster to the spare room they'd given me.

"What the fuck!" Jack shouted.

Frannie must've stopped him with a stern hand on his chest, but I wasn't looking over my shoulder to see.

"You just couldn't keep your hands to yourself for an hour or two, could ya?" I heard her say.

Next thing I knew, I was running straight to my room. I turned once to slam the door, and then again to crash down on the bed.

I buried myself there and cried myself to sleep.

"Hey, baby girl. Wake up."

In my dreams, I forgot about the agony of seeing him with that trashy whore. His words made me happy. I glowed, wishing he'd say something else.

Then I felt his hands shaking me gently by the shoulders. The happiness faded as I opened my eyes and realized it wasn't a dream.

I rolled over. Jack was sitting right next to me, that devilishly shy smile on his rugged face.

Raw emotion ripped through me. I wanted to be in his arms, but I also wanted him the hell out of my room after witnessing what he'd done.

"Go away," I sputtered.

"Not gonna happen. I need to know we're alright, Rach. I had a little too much to drink…never should've let that fucking slut on my lap. I regret it, even if upsetting you wasn't in the equation."

He sounded sincere. That bound the knots inside me tighter, turning them into neat little lumps. Confusion reigned.

I summoned the energy to face him again.

"You're the last person in the world I'd ever want to hurt. You've taken a lot of bullshit, Rach. I want to make it up to you…"

"Stop trying so damned hard," I snapped. "What you do is none of my business. If you want to sleep with blondie, be my guest. It's nothing to me."

That's a lie, I thought.

Jack laughed. All the turmoil in my words had done it. I didn't know what the hell I wanted, and neither did he.

Or so I thought.

He laid his hand on mine, wrapping my small palm in those powerful fingers. His touch was strong and soothing, even when it shouldn't have been. I fucking hated the way my body gave me away.

"It's my business to make sure you're comfortable here." He gazed into my eyes, never even stopping to blink. "It's near sundown. Do you want to go for a ride?"

"A ride?" I echoed, as if my brain refused to click to understanding his words.

"Yeah. On my bike. It's a beautiful evening. I'd rather blow out of here anyway before the kids go home and the guys get really rowdy. I haven't drunk myself so stupid I can't drive."

I hopped up, releasing his hand. Yeah, I was still halfway pissed at him over Michelle, but passing up a chance to ride on his motorcycle without danger nipping at our backs?

"Count me in," I said.

Jack gave me the biggest smile I'd seen. He pushed up off my bed and waved me to follow him. We wound through the party, blissfully unnoticed.

Michelle and the other whore must have retreated to the Purple Room. The door was closed, and muffled fuck noises were coming from behind it.

"Put your arms around me and hold on tight, baby girl. I'll take you through town and then we'll hit the open road for a bit. Feels good to get some of this fresh summer air."

He pushed a helmet with a little earpiece inside into my arms. I quickly put it on. When he saw I having trouble with the radio thingie, he smiled, and adjusted it gently on my head.

"There you be. Use this so we can talk to each other over the roar of this baby." He patted the bike for emphasis.

He wasn't kidding about that roar. I'd been too dazed and terrified during my first motorcycle ride to really appreciate how loud it got.

We left the garage and tore out of the compound, stopping just once so Jack could open and close the high automatic fence.

I was quiet for the first five minutes or so. Seeing Cassandra again brought mixed energy rushing through me, dark pasts colliding with my strange new present.

He guided the bike down the town's small main strip. I eyed the stores I'd been in a couple hundred times growing up.

Jesus. Did I really have a normal life once in this town?

"You seeing it yet, baby girl?" Jack's voice rang through the earpiece, surprisingly clear.

"Seeing what?"

"This town differently," he said. "You've got a whole new life here now. This place belongs to *us*, the real residents, not your fuck-heel of an old man or anybody else. As long as you're in this town under the club, I won't let anybody else dictate your life."

Anybody else? The possessive edge in his tone made me wonder if he'd be dictating my life from now on.

Something about that sent a warm current through my body. I wrapped my arms tighter around his waist, feeling his rock hard abs.

We blew out of Cassandra's little stretch in minutes, toward the prairie landscape I'd known my whole life. Nothing out here but hills and ranches, as far as the eye could see. We lived far enough from the oil boom so derricks and delivery trucks didn't taint our view.

"Hell of a sunset, isn't it?"

He wasn't kidding. A big orange fireball was halfway slipped beneath the horizon, hanging in the sky like a glowing pumpkin.

"It's beautiful. Been awhile since I really appreciated one like that."

"You're young," he pipped happily. "You're gonna see a lot of beauty, Rach. All the pretty things you need to outweigh the bullshit, long as you have somebody to keep them away."

"Is that you?" I was feeling courageous. Curious too.

He paused. "Just might be. You'd make a hell of an old lady, Rach."

I didn't say anything yet. Every surface of my skin lit with the same rosy warmth pouring from the sinking sun, crackling to the ends of my fingers, right where I touched his perfect body.

I wasn't ready to give up that easily. But the tighter I clung to Jack and the warmer his voice sounded, I thought I might one day.

"Tell me about the MC. I noticed some tension between you and your Dad at the party."

Jack looked over his shoulder for a second. His face was a little darker.

"Pop? Him and I have had our shares of disagreements about club business. Lately it just seems like he's giving up on shit. I don't like it. Gotta look alive in this business and remember what really matters, or else you'll get eaten the fuck up."

"This isn't because of me, is it?" I inhaled the cooling summer air slowly.

Another pause from him held the answer.

"I don't give a shit if it is. I don't regret taking you away from the Skulls for a single second. This club's had worse things happen before for far less noble causes. Maybe you're trouble, Rach, but only in Pop's senile brain."

"You sure?"

"I doubled down on you, didn't I? You're the kinda trouble I like." He laughed gently, a beautiful sound. "And I'm hoping to have a lot more of it soon."

So am I.

Bitch or no bitch, he'd won me back the instant we were on his bike. Feeling him beneath my hands just confirmed it. I rubbed my way up his chest, stifling a soft purr in my throat.

The animal part of my brain wished he'd jerk the bike up a country road, throw me in a ditch, and tear off my clothes.

Yep. I wanted him that fucking bad. I wanted him like nothing else, even if my whiny sane side wanted to pretend otherwise.

Maybe living with these bikers would be good for me. I'd let the good girl rule for almost twenty years. Wasn't it time to let the other Rachel out, the one Dad had always suppressed?

My hands snaked down his body, slipping just beneath his belt. He was hard all over.

"Easy where you move those little fingers, baby girl." His words were reluctant, heavy on his tongue, like he wanted to say the complete opposite. "Safety, you know."

I laughed at that. But maybe it wasn't so crazy.

The last thing we needed was to end up in a wreck from me toying with the bulge I knew I'd feel if I just let my hands keep going.

We rode into the lengthening darkness, talking all about old times in Cassandra. He told me about biker rallies in Sturgis, how he'd been part of the club his whole life.

I talked about happier times at the county fair and the way I'd always admired the Devils whenever they drove by. I intentionally stopped short of saying anything about my asshole father.

He always looked at the Devils with disdain. Called them criminals and 'low life scum.' How ironic that he'd gotten into bed with a pack of bastards way nastier than any Prairie Devils member.

By the time Jack turned around and started to head to the clubhouse, the stars were showing in the sky, bathing us in their pale silver light. If riding with him during the evening was glorious, then nighttime on the Harley with this man was downright magical.

"I'm so glad it's summer," I said. "Nice to be out at night admiring that view without freezing our asses off."

Jack nodded knowingly. "Yeah. Funny thing about stars is they're pretty familiar on my trips. Saw the same clear skies up in International Falls last week. They've always reminded me of home, the clubhouse, usually some shitty disaster going on that needs fixing."

"Oh…that's not very comforting."

"Always a mixed bag before. But riding with you tonight's changed all that. Now whenever I look up and I'm not here, I'm gonna think about you, baby girl. These are your stars up above."

He reached behind me and patted my thigh. I almost melted into a puddle behind him.

No man had ever talked to me like that before. I was starting to see why everybody called him Throttle.

His smile looked shy sometimes, but his words and actions definitely weren't. He powered forward. What Jack wanted, he laid claim to, and I had a feeling the next thing was going to be me.

Cassandra's antiquated lights went by in a blur. Before I knew it, we were pulling in through that high gate, unhooking our helmets in the hangar sized garage that housed all the club's vehicles.

I almost fell over when I climbed off the bike. Jack caught me, holding me close, guiding my eyes to his face with that gentle laughter.

"Sorry. Didn't think I'd be so dizzy."

"Just a little beginner's vertigo. You'll get plenty used to it. Can't wait until I take you on a longer trip. Maybe something that won't involve club business."

I'd like that. My heart throbbed, barely holding everything in.

The last thing I wanted to look like in front of him was the inexperienced blushing virgin I actually was.

"I'd better get inside. It's starting to get a little chilly." I squeezed him tight as I said the words.

"Not without this first." Jack leaned in, planting his lips hard on mine.

I never knew a kiss could burn. His heat started on my lips, hot and sweet and bright with electric desire, and then it swept south.

The wildfire blasted through me, setting all my nerves ablaze, every gentle movement in his lips quickening the fire. I went limp in his strong arms and moaned. My lips opened to the firm touch of his tongue, and then it was inside my mouth, raw and real.

The first time his tongue touched mine, I thought I'd die. He'd jolted me breathless and brainless. Parts I didn't want to acknowledge twitched with excitement, begging me to grind into him.

God, I almost did.

If it hadn't been for Warlock, I'm sure I would've given it up that very night.

"Hey, Throttle."

Jack broke the kiss at the sound of his words, shooting the furry senior member the most annoyed look in the world.

"What the fuck?"

"Didn't mean to interrupt." Warlock looked at me and I blushed, peeling myself away from Jack's warmth. "The Prez wants you in the meeting room to debrief on the trip. He really wants the skinny on whatever the fuck went down with the Canadians."

"It's okay." I whispered up at him. "I need to turn in anyway."

"You do that, baby girl." He ran his rough hand across my cheek one more time before looking at Warlock. "You coming, or what?"

"Nah, man," Warlock said. "Told me he wanted to talk to you alone."

"That just fucking figures. Okay, let's get her inside and get this shit over with."

I walked behind Jack with Warlock trailing me as we re-entered the clubhouse. Old seventies music was blasting out the jukebox, and the voices had died way down.

The whole clubhouse smelled like beer, cigarettes, and barbecue sauce. The pungent smell whacked me in the face, making it a little easier to make my way to my room.

"Have a goodnight," I said, stopping at my door.

Warlock nodded and kept going past me. Jack stopped and turned, aiming one more sultry smile my way.

"I already did. You rest up. Now that I'm back, I'm gonna do whatever it takes to turn things around here.

And nobody's gonna fucking stop me, especially where you're concerned."

I practically jumped into my room, slammed the door shut, and leaned on it. For the next hour before I collapsed in a dead sleep, I was in pure nirvana.

IV: Rightful Property (Jack)

I'd been close with bringing that heavenly angel to rock solid earth. *So fucking close.*

If it weren't for Pop, I would've had her in my bed, showing her how much I really cared. I wanted to back up my words with hard, sweaty action worshiping every sweet curve of her tight little body.

I wasn't sure what the hell I was thinking letting that slut get so close to me in the first place.

Both our whores have been eyeing me up and down for a good long while. Sure, I fucked them in the past when I was drunk and needed quick pussy.

What guy in this charter hasn't?

But seeing the razor sharp jealousy filling up Rach's eyes was something else. I didn't even feel bad about peeling Michelle off me like an old condom stuck to my shoe.

Seeing Rachel reminded me who I really wanted, who I fucking needed after everything that had gone down the last couple weeks.

I considered myself damned lucky that she'd taken me up on the evening ride. Having her hands pressed around my waist was hotter than a full romp with any woman I'd fucked before. And that kiss I stole on her plush young lips...fuck!

Just fuck!

My cock kept throbbing all night thinking about it. Too bad Pop pissed in my punchbowl.

Maybe it was good news for Rachel. Dealing with his shit was the only thing that held me back from breaking down her door and dragging her to my cave like my great-great-great-great-grandfather Unga-Bunga four thousand years ago.

Instead of having the best sex of my life, I was stuck in the stuffy meeting room, listening to Pop flapping his gums.

He wanted every little nitty-gritty detail. That's the way it looked, anyway, but I knew he was really just trying to keep me on my feet and remind me that he still held the gavel in this club.

"God damn it, son!" He bellowed at the climax of our meeting, slamming his huge wrinkled fists on the table. "Nobody controls what the Ontario boys do. They act on their own initiative, I get it. But you're a fucking idiot for egging them on, encouraging them to go after the Skulls south of the Maple Leaf."

"The Snakes have always been more proactive than this club. You know that, Pop. The second I told them there was a threat to our cross border business, they told me they were gonna take matters into their own hands."

"Bullshit." Pop glowered at me. "You got exactly what you wanted – turning a skirmish with those assholes into a full on war. I hope you're ready to reap what you sowed, son."

"Is there really any question? Seems like you're the only one who isn't ready to fight for our MC."

He stood up. Pain rippled across his face as he stood. His messed up spine wasn't getting any better.

"You say that to me again and I will have your reckless fuckery brought up for a vote. I know you think this gavel's automatically yours when I step down. Hell, I want it to be, but people aren't gonna listen to you if all you do is put their asses on the line for no good reason."

No good reason? Rachel's the best fucking reason for anything I've ever done on that bike.

Fuck you, old man.

I stopped just short of saying it to his face. Despite the bitter disappointment and exhaustion shining in his pale gray eyes, I loved him. What small shred of respect I had left saved me from saying the words that would guarantee he threw those old fists at my face.

"I told you about the deals, the Snakes, all the bullshit I saw up north. Is there anything else you want to know or what?"

Pop shook his head. Negative.

"Then I'm out."

It was easier to talk about leaving that conversation behind than doing it. Almost as hard as forgetting Rachel, ignoring the soft sweet tang of her sugar I still tasted on my lips.

I headed straight for the bar. I knocked back that whiskey I'd been missing earlier, enough to keep me drunk and blasted off my ass for the next twelve hours.

"Hey, big guy. Watch what you're doing with my baby girl."

I looked up from staring at the bar's scratched up countertop. Frannie slid into a seat next to me.

"I made it up to her. Told you she wasn't one to hold grudges," I said, reaching for the half depleted Jack bottle next to me. "Fill you up?"

Frannie nodded. I filled her glass to the brim and she kicked it down in one gulp. She clinked it on the counter and smiled sweetly, not even batting an eye.

That old lady could take booze better than most of my brothers.

"I'm warning you nicely, young Shields. I can't stand to see her hurt again after all she's been through. I'm an old lady. It's not my place to keep tabs on who you're fucking or throwing aside." She paused, sliding a little closer to me. "But if you're gonna fuck her, then it better lead to something."

"That's good advice."

It was. I wouldn't let on more than that, not to Frannie's face, and she expected as much.

"Hey!" I yelled and swatted after her as she ripped the bottle up into her arms.

"My old man needs to unwind after all this excitement tonight. Lord knows I do too."

She shot me a wicked grin over the shoulder, slowly making the way back to the club room she shared with Warlock.

I drank alone. A bunch of guys and their girlfriends were slumped in their chairs, deep in a drunken sleep.

I stepped over the two Prospects on the way to my room. Both of them were laid out flat on the dirty floor.

Had a feeling Freak and Tank were going to go far in the years to come. That is, if they put as much effort into their work as they did their partying.

I crashed in bed. After so much riding and tension this evening, my bones were like brittle wood. The whisky nipped at the edges of my brain, blunting the urge to fuck each time it surfaced.

Exactly how I wanted it. Resisting the urge to do something stupid like stagger into the Purple Room for a quick lay was a lot easier with a bad case of whiskey dick.

Good. Keeping numb for a little longer will keep me smart and pure for her.

Yeah, Frannie, I'll take your advice. Just wish I could tell you how bad I don't need to hear it.

The thought of *anyone* hurting that baby girl I wanted to stake a claim to filled me with a blinding rage. My eyes rolled red and black, straight through hate and love, gateways to the dark peace in deeper sleep.

Hold on, Rachel, I thought to myself, just before losing control. *Just a little bit longer. And then I'm coming for you, and you're never gonna have to worry about being lonely or unprotected ever again.*

"Throttle! Wake up, VP. We gotta fuck of a situation out here!"

What the fuck? Who was banging on my door this early in the morning?

Wasn't even noon yet. I jumped up, spitting a few choice curses when I felt the hangover pounding in my skull.

This better be abso-fucking-lutely important.

I almost tore the door off its hinges. Bolt was in front of me, his lips quirked at their sides in amusement.

"What?" I roared.

"It's that jackass Mayor. He's showed up here with a couple jackboots. Says he wants what's his."

That got me up. I shook off the hangover, suddenly light as a feather, stomping like a bull out of my room without even closing the door.

"Hey! Throttle!" Bolt yelled after me, racing to catch up as fast his lean legs would carry him.

"Where is he?"

"Out front. Main entrance by the garage. Figured you'd want to meet him where he can't add to the mess in here if things go sideways. Warlock's already out there with the asshole…"

I wasn't listening anymore. That horrible rage I had over anyone hurting Rachel before I drifted off last night?

Yeah, it was back, foaming up my body like lightning of an angry god.

I punched open the front door and ran down the steps. Mayor Fuck-face was waiting for me, looking all prim and proper in his dry cleaned suit and neat red tie.

Christ, how did such an ugly cocksucker create such a beautiful daughter? Rach must get everything from her mother.

Two guys in clean white uniforms were at his sides, standing like bulldogs. I recognized the stupid knock off patches fixed to their chests.

Hired mercenaries. Not real cops. Good, that should be less shit for the club if we ended up having to show the mercs who's boss.

"Mister Shields." Hargrove nodded at me, folding his hands behind his back. "I believe you have something that belongs to me."

I was about five feet away, and closing. Bolt stopped there next to Warlock, but I kept coming, and I had no intention of stopping either.

The Mayor jerked back just before I could ram my chest into his face. The two mercs threw their hands out, blocking my sorely needed progress.

"You better hope you don't say Rachel. If I hear you say her name, then I won't be able to stop what comes next. You've been warned…asshole."

Shit, it felt amazing to call him that to his face.

"Fine, be that way," he said, nervousness ringing in his voice. "Truth is, you have my daughter. I trust you've kept her well, but she can't stay. She doesn't belong here."

"She sure as fuck doesn't belong with you!" I jerked against the burly arms between me and the Mayor.

The bodyguards pushed back. In a flash, Bolt and Warlock were at my sides, ready to flatten them if they were stupid enough to throw the first punch.

"You're wrong, Mister Shields. She belongs with her loving father. Yes, Rachel and I have had our little disagreements, but she's still my daughter. You have five minutes to bring her out here, or I'll have my associates call the authorities. Obviously, she's not a minor, but I think any man with a badge will be sympathetic to a girl from a wonderful family who's been drugged and carried off by Cassandra's chief crime syndicate."

The venom in that prick's words…it cut deep and instantly set the wounds in my brain on fire. The fire in my fists and knees burned so bad I couldn't think straight anymore.

I started laughing. That got a quick look between Hargrove and his guards.

"I get it now," I said, shaking off a few last chuckles. "You brought these assholes to do the dirty work. Can't have Rach talking to the police herself now, right? Or else she might say something that could skull fuck your political career. You've been Mayor for – what? – a couple solid months now? That's a long time to hold office and still have Sheriff Bills looking at you like you just got barfed out of the sewer."

"I don't see anyone moving to get my daughter," he said coldly.

"How about now?"

I charged forward, busting right through the guards' linked arms. They threw themselves on top of me.

I was laughing as their weight vanished a second later, yanked away by my brothers. Warlock and Bolt let their fists fly. I listened to them exchanging fists with the mercs.

Hargove stood like a living cartoon with an *oh shit* plastered on his face. He turned and tried to run, but I was too fast.

I slammed him to the pavement, rolled him over, and pushed his flabby arms away as he tried to cover his nasty face. The heavy stones attached to my arms started to avalanche down.

I savored every fucking punch. My knuckles were hot and red within seconds, and still hungry for blood.

"No, no, no, no!" Every protest from his mouth got louder with each blow.

Soon, Hargrove was gurgling his words through blood. I knew I'd busted his lip and probably several teeth too.

He jerked beneath me, weak and helpless as a washed up fish. If it hadn't been for the Prospects, I would've split his skull clean open.

"What the fuck!" I screamed, as soon as I realized my fists weren't connecting with his face anymore.

"Pull him back!" Pop howled behind me. "Come on! We can't kill this bitch, much as I'd like to."

"Easy, easy, man. We're just trying to help, VP."

No, you guys are just following orders. Only kinda help I need is for you morons to hold him down while I finish making our Mayor into a raspberry smoothie.

Freak was pretty skinny. I could've shaken him off me if he were by himself, but Tank was on the other side. I was strong, but not as big and strong as our new bodybuilder-turned-Prospect.

"This is on you, Pop." I stopped thrashing. "I knew you wouldn't let me end this here. Too easy for you, old man."

"Your brain's in your ass, son." Pop didn't take his eyes off me as he lowered his face, moving his mouth near my ear. "What the hell do you think would happen if I let you murder the Mayor of our town at the clubhouse? Hm? You think you've got all the answers, Jack, but you don't know shit."

I jerked once, fighting my own brothers to get on my feet. I couldn't. Tank roared, struggling with Freak to keep me down.

"Can everybody walk?" Pop was talking to Warlock and Bolt now.

I lifted my head, grinding my teeth as I watched them reluctantly help up the bodyguards they'd just knocked flat.

Hargrove's boys were both limping. Mayor Fuck-face stayed down, and that brought a juicy smile to my lips.

Pissed me off that he was still breathing. But at least I'd done a real number on him.

"Get up. I know you can hear me," Warlock said. "We'll help you to your car, and then you're getting off our property. Don't be a dumb fuck, Mayor. You know what to do. Stay away from this club and don't ask about your daughter ever again. Understood?"

The Mayor groaned unintelligibly. Warlock and Bolt leaned down, picked him up, and slid him into the arms of the scratched up bodyguards.

All three men seemed to lean on one another for mutual support. Nobody looked worse than Hargrove with his hair messed up and blood smearing his face. A few fresh trickles had spotted the neat white shirt beneath the jacket, making it look like the tie in the middle was bleeding.

That's right, you fucking demon. Take a good look at me. Look at the man who's gonna finish the job he started if you ever show your ass around here again.

"Get them out of here and lock the place up," Pop said with disgust.

Warlock and Bolt trailed the intruders to the open gate, ready to slam it shut.

"Wait! Don't go yet!"

The high feminine voice broke the eerie silence. Everybody looked up in shock as Rachel appeared, watching us like a phantom on the ledge outside the door. She was wearing some long white skirt Frannie had found for her.

She sailed down the stairs. I watched her walk right past me, and that set me struggling against the Prospects again.

"Easy, VP. The girl's gotta do whatever she's gotta do." Freak tried to be soothing. He just ended up pissing me off.

Don't do it. Don't go up to your lunatic old man, baby girl.

The trio of Hargrove and his bodyguards stopped when they saw her. Warlock and Bolt stared at each other on both sides of the fence.

Everybody wondered what the hell was going down.

For a split second, I was horrified I'd have to break out and let myself get broken trying to reach her. Or, worse, let her do something stupid like follow that asshole to his Mercedes and climb in the backseat.

"Rachel? Come with me." Hargrove blubbered, slurring his words. "Let me take you away from these animals…"

Nobody – and I mean nobody – expected her to fling spit right in his face. But that's exactly what my brave girl did, spraying him right in his fucking bloodied face with a big string of wet saliva.

Half my brothers roared. The rest laughed.

She ran back to safety, back to us, before the asshole could even think about ordering his goons to do anything.

The guards had to drag him across the boundary separating the clubhouse from the public sidewalk. Then my brothers wheeled the gate shut, a hell of a lot faster than the automatic closing mechanism could.

"You vermin just made a big mistake. Big, big mistake! Do you fucking hear me?" The Mayor shouted, flinging his body against the fence like a loose puppet, before his guards pushed him into the back of the car.

The Mercedes sped off. A very shocked Rach returned to my side, her eyes shining.

"Come on. He's gone, guys, let me up."

Pop nodded. Tank and Freak peeled away and I hopped up on my feet.

"It's gonna be okay, Rachel. I don't give a shit what he says. He's never setting foot on this property again if he wants to keep breathing."

She threw herself into my chest. I held her tight.

Even with all the brothers watching and my own father, I didn't flinch. With her there, so close and so sweet, my world began at her soft hair and ended where her skirt flowed out at her knees.

Nothing else mattered. Nobody else did either.

"You really upset him. You know that, Rach?"

"Yeah. I've never heard him swear like that in my whole life," she said softly. "I just hope my spit burns those cuts you left on his face. I've seen him, and one last time is more than enough."

We were all gathered around the table. Some of us were staring at Pop, and the rest were looking past the club

President to the big black and white Prairie Devils banner hanging on the wall behind him.

The rough looking devil's face was neatly flanked by pitchforks on both sides. The old flag had hung in this room since I was a kid, something the boys threw up shortly after Pop and the original guys founded this MC.

"Hell of a way to start the morning, ain't it?" Jonesy gazed up and down the table at us, newly healed and back in action after his tango with the Skulls.

"Yeah, it is," Pop said quietly.

His eyes weren't on Jonesy, though.

Here it comes, I thought. *Asshole's gonna call a vote to have me struck down as VP. That evil eye he's giving me can't mean anything else.*

"This shit's gone too far. Way over the line. If we're gonna do this thing, then we need to make some serious fucking changes around here to whip us into fighting shape. That's your job, Jack." Pop raised one hand and pointed.

"What?" Color me genuinely surprised. I didn't know what the hell he was getting at.

"Get this club ready for war. Scorched earth. Nobody – and I mean *nobody* – comes crashing into my club with a list of demands out the wazoo. I'll wring Hargrove's fucking neck myself."

I smiled. That's the good old Pop I remembered, the one I thought had been buried.

Prideful, vengeful, and ready for blood if anybody threatened what was his. Despite all his faults, he was on my side this time, and I was gonna take whatever bone Lady Luck had thrown me and run with it.

"You want us to go after him?" Warlock looked just as shocked as I did.

"Does this place still smell like beer, barbecue, and pussy?" Pop said rhetorically. "We're gonna do it, but we're gonna do it smart. We need to find out what the Raging Skulls had on him to turn him into their bitch. Whatever skeletons there are in his closet, they're big enough to bury him."

I nodded. It was weird to find myself a hundred percent in agreement with Pop. It was the kind of weird I liked.

"Somebody did some research. Looked into his past. We need a guy to go after the right records, just like the Skulls, and hit that fucker in the face with his own dirty underwear." Bolt's eyes were bright with excitement, the wheels in his head doing overtime.

"Congratulations," I said. "Sounds like you just volunteered for book duty."

"Listen to the VP," Pop said. "Maybe the girl can tell us something that'll point us in the right direction. In the meantime, we need to get our defenses up and do patrols."

Everybody groaned. When the club went on red alert, groups of three or four were circling the immediate neighborhood all the time, an advanced scouting party looking for any trouble around the clubhouse's perimeter.

"Stop your bellyaching! There'll be plenty of time for whiskey and getting your dicks wet when this shit's behind us. There always is." Pop looked over, waiting for me to add to his wisdom.

"What about Rachel? We gotta keep her here for protection, but she can't stay in limbo forever. We need to make her an official part of this club."

Pop's jaw tightened. I saw the reluctance rising in his face. Maybe I'd just pressed my advantage too far, taking advantage of the opening with him.

I didn't care. I had to try, for her sake.

"Has the girl got any brains?"

I folded my arms, trying to hide my irritation. "Of course she does. She can learn anything we throw at her. Why, what the hell are you thinking?"

"Frannie needs to train her in on some basic first aide, and then the more advanced shit. Who knows what the Skulls and hired mercs have in store for us as soon as Hargrove gets his pecker back up. That fucker's gonna come here with a wrecking crew, and an extra set of hands to patch people up won't hurt."

The rest of the men glanced at each other coldly. They knew the stakes were high, just like I did, and it was all too easy to end up with a lot more than scrapes and scratches.

"I'll tell Frannie to train her in," I said. No hesitation.

Keeping Rachel here and valuable to the MC would keep her safe. The club wasn't intended to babysit or shelter for too long, but she'd have a proper home if she was working for the org, same as the rest of us.

"Everybody in favor of the girl staying permanently?"

Hands went up simultaneously. All my brothers said "aye," but nobody said it louder than I did. Pop's gavel hit the wood beneath it with a loud *clack!*

"Then it's settled. The girl's gonna stay on as an assistant nurse. Least she can do for stirring up all this shit."

I shot Pop a bitter glance. Damn it, I knew he wasn't gonna keep his cool forever without saying something guaranteed to piss me off.

"You boys meet Jack in the garage to hash out patrols and make sure all our equipment works. Remember, brothers, our friends could show up here with guns blazing at any second. I can't have a single man slacking on the fucking job. Got it?"

Another round of 'ayes' and nods. Pop pushed back his chair, relaxing his back, a signal to everybody else to get moving.

I was the last one out. Just before I closed the door behind me, our eyes linked up, and I saw the stern trust in his eyes.

"Don't let me down, son. You're getting your way this time because it's the right thing to do. Show me and the club that you're fit to lead this MC."

"When we beat Mayor Fuck-face and the Skulls, you're gonna see how wrong you were, Pop. You never had any reason to doubt me."

I stepped away, slamming the door behind me.

It took all fucking day to get everything in order with my brothers.

By late evening, everybody who wasn't on patrol was in the bar, drowning their worries in liquor and tobacco. I saw Warlock and slid into the bench next to him.

"I told Frannie to get going on Rachel's lessons. You'll be happy to hear she was falling all over herself to learn. Don't think she's had a purpose like this for a long time."

I smiled. My older and wiser brother was right.

Having some meaning felt good, and I knew giving Rachel a little responsibility would go a long way toward undoing the damage her sick daddy did. Everything I knew about her said he'd brought her up like sheltered eye candy.

Well, as far as I was concerned, the photo ops, arranged associations, and family secrets were over. Rachel belonged to the MC now, her new home, and soon she'd belong to me too. Once the club was open, it gave as much as it got.

We were brothers and sisters, fathers and daughters, with ties thicker than blood. Especially blood that turned on itself like Rach's demented old man.

I'd make sure this beautiful dove mended her wings and took flight. With me at her side, she'd rise up like a phoenix, so strong and bright it hurt to even look at her.

"Thanks. She's gonna be amazing," I said, no longer hiding the smile creeping across my face. "How you holding together with all this?"

Warlock shrugged. "Nothing this club hasn't dealt with before. I remember the big war with the Ass Busters from Wyoming. Almost fifteen years ago now, back when you were just a little shit. We lost a lot of good guys busting their asses on the highway outside Minot…"

Warlock had that thousand yard stare. He'd never been in the military like Pop, but he'd seen more shit than most soldiers.

Those old photos in the hallway were a testament to how many good men the club had lost earning its place in the world. Guys I remembered, some only vaguely, haunted those photos like ghosts in black and white.

Truth is, clubs like the Devils can't be anything but wolf packs that look after their own and flip the rest of the world the fucking bird. We were modern knights, made to wade through fire, blood, and steel on those growling steeds we rode.

The older I got, the easier it was to understand why Pop had turned into such a no nonsense hardass. He knew if our club let down its guard, even for one second, a gang of upstarts would muscle in our territory and turn everything upside down.

I wouldn't let them piss on the graves of everybody who fell wearing our colors. Neither would anybody else who wore the Prairie Devils' patch.

We couldn't quit, couldn't relax for even a second. We had to keep riding straight into the storm, hardening our bodies with the same fearless, uncaring energy that powered our bikes.

"We're better off with your experience, brother." I slapped Warlock on his meaty shoulders. He managed a small smile through the painful memories.

"Better old and useful than dead and useless," he said. "Or too beaten up to do anything but suck booze through a tube and vote by proxy."

"You'll never be obsolete, man. Hell, guys like you are the reason we fucking suffered and bled, but came out stronger today. It's no secret Pop gets under my skin a lot of the time...but he manages to come to his senses. You older guys are the hard nails keeping this ship together. We're gonna punch through all this latest shit, same as we always do."

"No doubts here," Warlock said, turning his half-drained vodka tonic in one big hand. "Just hope we don't have to bury more of our own after we've buried every last fucker on their side."

"We won't. Trust me, brother. If any one of us ever dies on my watch in combat, then I haven't been doing my job."

I really believed my words. I'd been through big skirmishes, but always under Pop's command until the last couple years, when he directed most of our battles from behind the lines.

All the responsibility for casualties had been his. Now that I was in charge in most of the big firefights, all that shit was piled up on my shoulders, heavy as a giant boulder.

I was damned determined to keep it from getting away and rolling over us.

Warlock wished me a goodnight, got up, and staggered back toward the room he shared with Frannie. Excitement flickered in my blood as I sat at the bar a little longer, knocking back my whiskey in one shot.

The warm glow bristled like fire in my almost empty belly. I needed that heat now for what I was about to do.

The day had turned out ten times crazier I than expected, but I wasn't done yet.

I still had something I absolutely, positively had to cross off my bucket list. I got up, blood burning like lava, and made a direct line for Rachel's room.

"Fuck," I muttered to myself.

My baby girl wasn't there. I found her a couple rooms over, in the infirmary. At least Frannie wasn't wasting any time getting her up to speed on medicine.

I pushed the door open and lingered out of sight, listening to her sweet voice asking questions. She was going to do an amazing job when crisis hit. Rachel's interest burned bright, just like her instructor's.

"Let's go over it again, hon. How do you tell when someone's in shock?" Frannie sounded just like a pro.

"Weak pulse, shallow breathing, clammy skin, unfocused eyes and…um…vomiting sometimes?" Rachel rattled it off perfectly until the end.

"Only sometimes. Don't let the obvious things like bleeding and vomiting bog you down, girl. You need to jump right in and check the vitals. They tell the real story."

"Got it."

They both looked up when I stepped around the corner. I braced my hand on the big steel table we'd installed for serious shit sometime ago, courtesy of an old clinic that shut down a couple towns over.

"You done overloading her brain for one night?" I aimed a big smile in Frannie's direction.

She cocked her head, pushing her hands on her hips. "Give her a little more credit. For someone who decided to pass on college, she's got awesome focus."

"Yeah!" Rachel piped up. "I'm not an idiot. It's easy to pay attention because all this stuff is really interesting."

"I'm sure it is," I said, raising my hands to my chest as mock shields. "I didn't even understand half the shit you guys were talking about. That's why we leave the medical nitty-gritty to you ladies. No brother here has the patience to sit down and sort this shit out."

"Thanks for finally getting me another set of hands," Frannie said. The smile on her lips said she really appreciated it.

"It was Pop's decision, but you better believe I supported it. Just watch out, Frannie. Only a matter of time before she's doing most of the leg work around here. I hear it's easier when you're young and spry."

Rachel laughed. Frannie stuck her tongue out at me.

"She can have at it. I'm tired of getting my hands all covered in spit and blood every time one of you guys steps into it."

"Spit?" Confusion crossed Rach's face.

"You wouldn't believe the way these big tough bikers blubber like babies when they're hurt. Sometimes for good reason. But usually they're crying over tetanus shots and a splash of alcohol on their scraped knees."

Everybody laughed. Then that eager fire switched on again, filling my blood, spurring me to get on with what I'd come to do.

"Seriously, I need to have a chat with Rach. Can she break for the night?"

Rachel turned toward her mentor with saucer sized eyes. Frannie took one look at the excitement in her eager student's face and nodded.

"Go on. Just don't keep her up too late," Frannie said knowingly. "We're gonna pick up on this again tomorrow in the early afternoon. I'll give her the night plus tomorrow morning to let some of the info sink in. Oh, and here!"

Frannie reached to the opposite counter. Grunting, she picked up four big textbooks and shoved them in Rachel's direction.

I instantly stepped in, giving Rach a *no-you-fucking-don't* look. "Help you carry these anchor weights to your room?"

"I'd like that," she said softly.

Fuck, the smile on her face…pure heat throbbed inside me from the waist down. All my muscles were begging to lay into her, and I had to look away to keep my whole body from seizing up.

Soon, soon. Keep it the fuck together, man. Last thing I need to do is embarrass myself like a gawky fucking teenager.

I scooped up the books. We each wished Frannie a goodnight and left the infirmary, heading straight for her room.

Tonight, with any luck, the last little star was about to fall in this angel's life. Mine too.

I'd had it up to fucking here with all these crazy distractions. If I had to, I'd nail the door shut and throw boards over the windows to keep the rest of the world the fuck *out*.

There was no more room for anything else. Tonight, it was just me, Rachel, and an old bed I hoped would be able to take the pounding we were gonna give it.

Just a few more steps baby girl. Then you're mine, and I'm never, ever gonna let you go.

V: Like a Gritty Fairytale (Rachel)

My heart was pounding when I opened the door. My hand shook as I reached inside, switched on the lamp, and quickly threw myself inside to make way for him.

Him! Jack's in my room now, and for once it's not about some club bullshit or making up for dumb mistakes.

Today, the hungry glint in his eyes told me there was only one thing he was after.

The door clicked shut and I threw the lock. The mechanism had a loud finality, as if it meant to seal us inside another world.

"Over there," I said.

I pointed to the small table where I kept a couple old romance books Frannie had given me. Jack leaned over the short table, giving me a lovely view of that rock hard ass he carried so well beneath his jeans.

He turned and looked at me, wearing his trademark shy smile. Or maybe not-so-shy today?

Old floorboards creaked beneath his feet as he stepped closer, bridging the last distance between us.

"Romance, huh? Didn't realize you were such a bookworm."

"Just something to keep the mind busy. I like to read, but it isn't my favorite thing in the world."

Jack was only inches away from me. I stared up into his big dark eyes. They completely sucked me in until I was lost in them. He left me awestruck, strangely curious about all the mysteries wrapped around this beautiful man.

"I had a feeling you'd say that, baby girl." He pushed his forehead against mine, stamping my lips with his hot breath. "Reading's no substitute for the real thing. Aren't you curious what a real man is like?"

Holy shit, holy shit…

My brain just shut down. His hands went to my low back, and then sank lower. He cupped my ass and squeezed, pulling me into him.

The bulge tenting the middle of his jeans pressed close. Sweat sizzled on my brow. I temporarily forgot how to breathe.

"I'm curious, yeah. Especially if that man is you."

I lifted my eyes slowly to his. Hunger steamed in the stars lining his pitch black pupils, tiny pinpricks as sharp and hot as lust itself.

"Don't you wonder any longer, Rach. Let me show you…"

He moved in for a kiss. I thought I was ready, but nothing truly prepared me for the hot, wet bliss of his wandering lips.

I moaned into his mouth, louder when his hands tightened on my ass. Jack kissed me deep, winding his tongue with mine, moving his lips in a steady, hypnotic pulse on my little inexperienced lips.

Excitement boiled up, bright and hot and addictive.

Through my daze, I noticed he was pushing me toward the bed, stopping to gently tap his knees on my legs when I reached the edge. He broke his kiss, sliding his calloused hand over my face, pouring more humid breath onto my cheeks behind it.

"Fuck. I can't wait any longer, baby girl. Let me unwrap you so we can do this thing. I've wanted to get you naked and tangled since the second I laid eyes you..."

More kisses. I was shaking in his arms, but he steadied me, a mountain of a man growing hotter by the nanosecond.

His hands edged my shirt, lifting up. He rolled it halfway to my breasts, exposing my naked skin pocked with goosebumps.

I froze. There was something I had to tell him, before he really rendered me speechless.

"Wait. Wait, wait...there's something you need to know." I swallowed hard.

I didn't want to tell him and expose my immaturity. But this rock hard man deserved to know what he was getting by taking me as a lover, even if it meant he might not want me at all.

But men like virgins, right? I hoped everything I heard was true. Like, really, *really* fucking hoped, sending a silent prayer up high.

"I've never done this before, Jack. I'm a virgin."

The smile on his face melted. It scared me at first, but that deeper, much hotter heat on his skin didn't lie. It was like his body temperature had gone up a few degrees.

Would he burst into flames and take me with him? God, I wanted him to.

"No fucking way." He shook his head.

"Are you serious?" He ran his hand to my jawline and stopped, spreading it to hold my chin.

"I wouldn't lie to you." I nodded, loving the raw masculine feel of his palm on my softness.

"Baby girl, you just made my day, my week, my whole fucking year. I'm gonna teach you so much, and it's gonna be amazing."

I moaned in agreement. The heat lining my skin developed into a full on blush. It was hell confessing to him, but heaven now that the big secret was out.

"Kiss me again, and then take off my shirt."

The look in his eyes said he wasn't offering anything. This was a command I had to obey, however rough and pleasurable that might be.

I tensed my hands around his back, fingering the edge of the t-shirt he wore beneath his jacket. His shoulders rolled, pushing away his leather and letting it fall to the floor.

Jack pushed onto my lips for another kiss, and brought his hands to mine. He helped me lift his shirt away, high over his head.

I didn't dare look until he withdrew his lips. Just one glimpse of his bare chest and I was guaranteed to lose it.

And I did. My eyes wandered slowly up his rock hard abs, stopping at the devil's face tattooed across his breasts. It was just like the big patch on their jackets. On each bicep he had matching pitchforks.

He lived, breathed, and wore the MC's symbols. Now, it looked like they empowered him too.

He was a slab of total strength, muscles fused together into tight dark canyons, all the way from his abs to those bulging biceps on each side. He pushed himself into me, encouraging my hands to go higher.

Smiling, Jack turned, exposing his back. It was cut just like the rest of him, muscular and broad.

Between his shoulders, he wore one giant pitchfork. The words *Prairie Devils MC* were stamped in dark ink below it. So was another phrase.

The road forgets. Devils don't.

"What's that all about?" I asked, gingerly touching the ink. "The road forgets?"

"Yeah. You can hop on the nearest highway and become a whole new person. You'll be forgotten sooner or later by your shitty job, your friends, your family. But if you wear these colors or live under them, then you're part of the MC forever, and the club never forgets."

"Never?"

"Hell no. That goes for our members, our friends, our enemies, and even our old ladies. You give respect, you get it. You shit on us, and we won't take the heat off until you're nothing but ash."

A chill went through me. It was easy to forget that this handsome warrior was part of a group that was so feared.

Feared, and respected.

He was taboo in all the ways family and society warned me about. Off limits. Except just now, he wasn't. He was within my reach – all of him – the kind hearted Adonis and the violent outlaw.

"Is it the same with you?" I asked.

"Fuck yeah, it is. Except I can give a lot more than respect to those who deserve it. I can deliver love, and all kinds of good things with this body that won't ever stop."

I steeled my eyes and took a good look at him. He wasn't lying. I reached out, reaching for his tats, the inks that invited me to slowly run my nails across his divine surface.

He exhaled hard, slowly, clearly enjoying my touch.

"Fucking A. You have no idea what you do to me, do you, baby girl?"

I was too deep in man candy to answer. He turned, faster this time, and wrapped me in a tight embrace.

Jack's moment of slow, sensual tolerance had ended. The beast inside him surfaced, and his fingers went for the shirt he'd started to lift before.

Oh, God. Please don't let my looks fail me now...

I tensed as he undressed me, guiding me down on the bed as soon as my shirt was off. Jack covered me, finding his place between my legs, planting more fiery kisses on my skin.

He started on my neck, flicking out his tongue for an extra tease, pushing his lips in a steady trail to my cleavage. When he reached the place between my breasts, he cupped them in both hands, pulling gently at the bra and sucking hot skin between his teeth.

I arched up into him, groaning like a cat in heat. Just then, I absolutely was, and I wanted him to finish what he'd started – even if it meant I was going to burn until I blacked out.

"Grab my shoulders and pull yourself up, baby. Time to show me those beautiful tits."

I did as he asked. He slid his hands behind my back and popped my bra's clasp.

How many times had he done this? There was no hesitation, no fumbling like a younger boy would.

That made me burn even hotter, realizing I was with a *man* who had experience and real need behind his desire.

Jack flung my bra over his shoulders and released the breath he'd been holding in, bathing me in hot air again. "Oh, fuck. You're more perfect than I imagined."

His hands roamed over my breasts. He caught my nipples between his thumbs and fingertips, squeezing them, plumping the hard buds for his mouth.

I started shaking when I saw his lips going to my right breast. The same wicked mouth that made me burn with his kisses sent more fire quaking through me when he sucked at my nipple.

"Jack! That feels..."

Fucking amazing, I wanted to say, but I was too deep in pleasure to finish my thought.

Lightning zipped up my spine. I'd never, ever felt anything like it, not in the naughtiest fantasies I'd had at Dad's house.

Probably because I never imagined a lover this hard, tattooed, and immaculate.

Jack rolled forward, pushing his bulge to my crotch. He rubbed me there, pushing me deeper into the bed, holding my nipple between his teeth and flicking his tongue across it again and again.

God! How embarrassing would it be if I came just from having him suck me like this?

I tried to keep the moaning, the shaking, the creaming under control. It was no use.

Sweat peppered every little corner of my body. My panties were ruined, and he hadn't even gotten my pants off yet.

Jack moved to my other nipple, working it over with the same wild energy as before. My body was learning, but it hadn't hardened to his touch. I gasped and moaned and shifted my hips all over again, flushing when I realized I was dry humping him.

Fuck! That's instinct taking over. Severing what little control I have left...

Something about that evil realization was wonderful.

My flesh was absolutely crawling by the time he finished teasing my breasts.

Jack tugged at my belt. I looked up, locking eyes with him, lifting my legs over his back as he tugged my jeans away.

Nothing between him now but those sopping wet panties. His eyes dropped, staring at the wet spot in the middle.

He bared his teeth. The beast behind all that tattooed muscle inhaled my scent, devoured my presence, totally driven to take me hard.

I shuddered. His fingers slipped beneath my waistband. He had a good grip and he pulled, tearing them down my legs. They hooked around one ankle and he balled them up, throwing them somewhere far away.

"Lift your legs, baby girl. Yeah, just like that. Keep 'em over my shoulders. You think you've felt what my tongue can do, but you've got no fucking clue..."

Nothing prepared me for the kisses on my thighs. His arms locked on my calves and held me on his shoulders, kissing his way forward, totally relentless.

I whimpered and felt my face turn scarlet. Oral sex filled me with a mad self-conscious heat, but nothing about the way he buried his face there said he was disgusted.

Quite the opposite.

Jack threw himself into me, right between my legs, sliding his tongue up my wet folds. He growled, sending a sharp vibration through my flesh.

The raw hunger turned me on even more, but it was no match for feeling his lips, his tongue, his teeth in my most sensitive place. His tongue shot out, fucking in and out my shallow opening, then glided up through my folds.

Holy, holy, holy fuck! I can't...take...anymore!

My brain was an oozing, overheated mess. His licks slowed, prolonging the delicious agony, making a slow and steady crawl to my clit.

I knew he was close. I started to pant like crazy. None of the oxygen I took in was satisfying my lungs, and my body knew there was just one cure.

"Oh, God! Jack, I –"

I fucking gave it up the instant his tongue flicked against my clit. One little tap became a full on smothering, wiggling lick.

Orgasm punched me above the waist. My womb contracted, convulsed, imploded on itself, shooting pinprick needles up my spine and into my head.

Screaming, I rocked against him, clawing at the sheets beneath me. My toes pinched against his tattoos, bent at an angle so unnatural it should've been torture.

Maybe this whole fucking thing was some depraved torment. But if it was, then it was the best pain I'd ever experienced in my life, the pain of becoming a grown woman and a barbarian's lover.

I came hard. Spasm after spasm wracked my whole body, pulling me deep into a special kind of darkness.

It was peaceful, warm, and alive with love. The kind of place where nothing could ever go wrong.

"Can't get enough of your sweet taste, baby girl," he said.

It sounded like his voice was a million miles away. I cracked my eyes open, wondering how long I'd been knocked out in post-orgasmic bliss.

"Luck for you I've got other appetites. Come on, Rach." He pulled me up by the hand, until I joined him on my knees. "I want to see your little mouth wrapped around my cock."

Wet heat flared between my thighs all over again. He held me gently, pushed out his hips, and I looked at the massive bulge in his jeans.

"Do it." He looked at me, then straight down, and nodded. "I'll help you."

My hands were shaking as I reached for his zipper. God, I'd never seen a real penis before in the flesh, and Jack's promised to be overwhelming.

It was a strange pleasure undoing someone else's clothing. When his button and zipper were finished, I pushed his jeans down, exposing the sleek black boxers underneath.

Jack moved his hands down his hips. The boxers snapped down, and a great big cock popped out, hard and throbbing for attention.

"Put your pretty face here and suck. Just like you're tasting the sweetest sucker in the world." His hand went behind my sinking head, guiding me to the tip.

I opened my lips wide and sampled his swollen head. It seemed as good a place as any to start. He tasted salty, warm, but mostly just hot, hot, hot.

I tried to go low, as far as I could. Actually, it wasn't very far at all, but on the way back up my tongue caught the ridges on his underside.

He stiffened, releasing a raspy growl. I pushed my tongue deeper in his flesh, following the groove around his crown.

"Ah, fuck," he whispered. "Fuck! Do more, baby girl, a whole lot more. You're so fucking warm and tight. Every lick's getting me ready to slide inside you…"

Thinking about him taking my virginity put an extra spring in my tongue. I licked harder, deeper, bobbing my head and loosening my jaw to take more of him.

One hand cupped his balls, gingerly touching the soft sack. I imagined the potent sap churning inside and moaned.

Around and around and around I sucked, tongued, and swirled.

Jack grunted, fisting my hair. He started to thrust slowly into my mouth, controlling how much of him I took, just when I was afraid I'd screw up and choke.

Every time I heard him sigh, a new tingle ran through me, heightening the current in my blood. His pleasure became sharper, and I wondered if he was about to blow.

"That's good, Rach. Really fucking good." He tugged me by the hair, gently moving my head off his cock.

Why did he make me stop?

"Get underneath me and spread your legs, little virgin. Now that you've got me all warmed up, it's time to fucking claim you just like I've been wanting to."

I had to fight to shift into position. It felt like my arms and legs had become stone beneath his ferocious gaze.

"You ready to have me shoved up inside you?" His whisper poured into my ear, hot and energetic.

"Fuck! Yes!" I hissed the words, blushing as the F-bomb slipped out. His cock pressed against the thin landing strip above my slit, teasing away the last remnants of my sanity.

"Do it, Jack. Take me. I want this so, *so bad.*"

He nipped at my neck and then pulled away. I watched him bend beneath the bed, quickly gathering his jeans. When he returned, he had a condom packet in hand.

His strong fingers tore at the foil and lifted out the rubbery sheath. I appreciated his calmer head, especially when I'd been all ready to take him inside me bare without a second thought.

Lust did frightening things. I wondered what it would be like when I finally fucked him.

Jack rolled the condom onto his length and tugged it snug around him. Even cloaked in dark latex, his length still looked damned sexy, poised to burrow into soft flesh like mine and fuck deep.

His hips moved against mine. He planted his big hands next to my head, leaning down to me, touching his cock to my aching core.

This time was different. This time, he wouldn't stop, even if I begged.

This man promised to turn into a machine, an animal, as soon as he got inside me, and there was no off switch, no taming him. Not unless I was completely ravaged, leaving us both slick and exhausted and spent.

Jack bared his teeth, releasing a pent up growl as he shoved forward. My eyes and lips popped wide open at the same time, electrified by the sensation of his thick cock splitting me open.

His length tunneled in through my slickness, deep and filling. Something weak tore at my entrance. It didn't burn as bad as I expected.

Rather, all the discomfort was coming from his size. He tore into me, forcing my body to adapt to his hard thickness. My flesh was learning to match his, to grow wetter and softer and become completely open to him.

Jack slid low, until I felt his balls mashed against my ass. He held himself there for a moment, lowering his torso, blowing hot air across to my lips until I was completely smothered in every beautiful inch of him.

"I could make love slow and sweet, but neither of us want that right now," he whispered. "I'm going to show you how to satisfy a man. Same way you set yourself on fire. Pay attention, baby girl, this is how you really fuck."

His cock jerked back up and then slammed into me, harder and faster. My whole body shook. I whined loudly, instinctively wrapping my arms and legs around his muscular body.

Somehow, I knew this was going to be one wild ride, and I'd be better hold on for dear life.

He'd given me a minute to ease into it. But I understood, he couldn't keep the beast chained up forever. Now that demon was out, rampaging into me, slamming his hips into mine again and again with a savage tempo I was beginning to love.

"Yes! Yes, yes, yes," I sputtered. "Use me rough. Teach me every dirty thing you know. *Please*, Jack."

He grunted a reply. His face stretched, exposing his surprise. He was shocked at what a little whore I'd become wriggling beneath him. So was I.

I guess too many years of holding it in had ruined me. With this perfect man between my legs, I wanted to let it all out. I needed to unleash my beast and let it frolic with his.

Every thrust took away a little more of the initial pain. The fire shifted, becoming mostly pleasure, and it let me drive my hips up to meet his thrusts.

My small cunt sucked and swallowed his fullness. Our flesh slapped together, steady music punctured only by the shrill whimpers leaving my lips.

Holy, holy fuck. I knew it would be good, but I never imagined this, never anything this intense.

And the intensity was only growing. That fireball that always came before orgasm kept getting bigger and bigger near my womb, braising all the muscles around it.

It was like my whole body was being stretched the longer he fucked me.

His thrusts came quicker. Jack hammered all the way to my womb, making me massage every rock hard inch of him. He grunted with satisfaction when he slammed into me, seeing the aftershocks moving my breasts.

"Come on this cock, little angel. Come hard and free like a woman now. Let it the fuck out!" His eyes rolled in his head, bleary with obscene passion.

The words just amplified his thrusts. They kicked me over the ledge, releasing the heatwave in my belly to go nova.

I came. Hard and fast and lightning hot, everything imploded, sucking hard at his length as he kept fucking through the wet velvet constricting around his cock.

I pinched my arms and legs around him before ecstasy blacked me out. He pounded my soft body up and down into the mattress, smashing my breasts into his powerful chest.

Old springs creaked beneath us, but they were no match for the wild screams echoing through the room.

Halfway through coming, Jack reached to my hips and cupped them in his fiery hands. He held me even tighter, pulling my ass up to him, forcing me to really feel every wonderful twitch of his cock.

Without warning, he added an extra swivel to his hips each time he thrust deep. My clit ground on him, sending new lightning streaking through my nerves.

This man, this master, prolonged my climax. I literally believed it might last forever before the tsunami inside me waned to softer waves, leaving me sore and breathless.

I realized he was fucking me faster than before as ecstasy released me from its grip.

Men weren't supposed to last this long, were they? Would I be able to keep up with his insane stamina?

Jack showed no signs of slowing down. If anything, he was getting hotter, more frantic.

He released my ass, pummeling me into the mattress again. His breathing hitched, and I had a feeling he wanted to blow, but he was holding back, enjoying erasing every last trace of my virginity.

"You want me to come, don't you, baby girl? You're so fucking tight, so good, I just might do that." His voice was tense. Strained.

"Yes." He'd read my mind. "Show me what it's like, Teach. Let go and give me your beautiful come."

I teased him with my words. Hell, I teased myself.

For a split second, I forgot he was wrapped up in that condom. Something deep and primal inside me ached to feel his come shooting up my womb.

Someday.

His hips shifted again. I gripped him tighter, locking my arms and legs around his muscular bulk. My ankles sank into his sides so hard they hurt.

Pleasure began ripping through me again at an alarming rate. He raised his pitch, his pressure. Neither one of us was going to last like this.

We were heading straight for meltdown, and it was fucking incredible.

"Kiss me goodbye, Rach. One last sweet little kiss before I –"

I nipped at his mouth. His lips smothered mine, pushing them back in their place. Adding teeth and tongue, he devoured, filling me at both ends with wicked desire.

I started panting as he broke the kiss. I couldn't move anymore, couldn't breathe. All I could do was hold on tight as he spiked deep one last time, planting his cock against my womb.

Feral notes ripped out of his mouth. Jack's head snapped back and his face contorted into a mask of pure pleasure.

His cock swelled inside me. I instantly came when he exploded through that latex.

Pumping, grunting, grinding, we came together. We shared our hearts, our souls, our bodies. In that beautiful moment, nothing – absolutely *nothing* – was held back.

Orgasm pulverized the walls between us, baring our hearts with such a wild openness it scared me.

I wanted to laugh and cry and hold him simultaneously. But all I could really do with his cock jerking inside me was clench with all my might, taking his explosion, sharing him like I'd never shared another human being.

I think I blacked out again when the heat became too much.

Next thing I knew, Jack's face was back to normal. He gingerly kissed the sweat and tears away from my face, rocking me against his powerful body. He stayed rooted in me, a little softer than before, pushing one hand through my tangled hair.

"How'd you like being claimed, baby girl? There's no going back after this."

"No?" My words sounded like they were a million miles away.

"No fucking way. This hair, this soft skin, this pretty little ass," he moved his free hand to one buttock and squeezed. I moaned. "It's mine. All mine, baby, and I'll keep leaving my mark on every inch so you never forget it."

Fuck. I'm game for anything with you.

I didn't tell him that, but I knew my body betrayed me. I was already getting hot and wet just thinking about how bad he wanted me.

I sighed with sweet relief and more than a little regret when he pulled out. Jack tossed the used condom into the waste bin across the room and cradled me tight.

We kissed softly and made small talk.

Perfection upon perfection. I hooked my chin into his shoulder and moved my face against his, loving the way his long stubble scratched at my skin.

Before Dad threw me into this world, he'd raised me to be his little Princess. I was supposed to go away and marry some snot nosed shit who'd give our family's political connections a leg up.

Even in my wildest dreams, I never imagined I'd end up an old lady to an outlaw on wheels.

But the years of fantasy were over the instant Jack Shields took my virginity and stole my heart. He carried me to a different kind of world, dark and rough around the edges, but beautiful nonetheless.

And no matter how sharp, how black, it was the one that was right for me because *he* was in it.

"Kiss me again, Jack. Just to remind me I'm not dreaming."

He lifted his smiling face to mine and gave me what we both wanted. When he pulled back, he held himself close, running his lips over mine a second time.

"I'll do you one better than a kiss, Rach. I'll fuck you, and then again and again after that. I'll fuck your sweet body until you can't ever fuck anybody else. You'll only mold to me. When I get what I want, baby, I don't ever let go."

And he was just as good as his word.

It was the longest, most sleepless night of my life. When the alarm on my phone bolted us up around noon, exhausted and red eyed, we just laughed.

What we'd only started sharing was completely worth it. I'd sacrifice sleep and a whole lot more for this man, this new keeper of my flesh.

The only man who deserved it.

VI: Slip Up (Jack)

"Throttle, man…you listening?" Bolt ran a hand through his hair, concern showing on his face that he was gonna have to repeat himself again.

Thinking about Rachel took every waking minute when I wasn't with her. Or it would've, if I didn't have all this shit to manage. Pop had me moving my guys around like a small army to lock down our clubhouse-turned-fort.

Fuck, I almost wish I knew I wasn't seeing her tonight. Almost. But she's coming to my bed for the first time, and I'm gonna drive her fucking scent into it.

I want to eat, breathe, sleep, and live my baby girl. That's all I want.

"I heard you. Just give me those details one more time about the new grenades."

Bolt looked at me sideways. If I weren't the VP, he would've made a smart assed comment, and he would've been entitled to. But then I would've had to beat his ass.

He picked up a small black canister in one hand and held it out. "Yank the pin, hold this tab on the side, and when you're ready to let loose, throw that baby right where you want it!"

Bolt let the grenade go. I ducked for cover, grabbing the laughing idiot and flattening him to the ground.

I held him there and waited. After thirty seconds, there was no explosion. I sat up.

"Jesus Christ! What the fuck are you doing?"

"It's a dummy, Throttle. A little something those Russkies gave us for demonstrative purposes when we bought the latest cache through the Canadians."

Bastard. I gave him a good whack in the arm. Hard enough to hurt, but not to do any serious damage.

"Ow!" Bolt jerked away from me and rubbed his bicep. "Guess I deserved that."

"You're not shitting." I helped him stand up and put some distance between myself the armory. "What else is on the agenda?"

"We're supposed to inspect the fallback point. Ready when you are, boss." He gave me a big shit eating grin.

Fucking A. I need to get it together and put the baby girl on hold for a micro-second. Last thing I need is my own brothers losing respect for me over pussy...

But she wasn't just pussy. Even as Bolt and I fixed our helmets and started our bikes, she was on the brain, reminding me she was so much more than a wet hole to fill.

Delicate, fresh, and beautiful. Hauling her pretty ass to bed the last few days excited me like nothing else. Rach made me feel more alive in less than a week than I'd been in the last ten years.

"Let's go," I said over the little radio clipped to my ear.

"Roger."

We peeled out the gate, tearing through Cassandra's streets and heading for the small older neighborhoods on the other side of the highway.

Jonesy's house stood out with overgrown weeds and chipped paint. I shook my head when I pulled up. Damn it, I didn't want to tell anybody how to live, but we didn't need to draw attention to this place.

Bolt cocked his head and looked at me, climbing off his bike.

"What's up?"

"Our brother still hasn't cleaned up after himself. I get that he's been taking it easy and recovering, but this is too much."

Shit. That was an understatement. This place was a fucking pigsty!

The front yard was even worse. Some miscellaneous tools and an old Harley without its wheels were lined up in the tall grass.

Bolt was at my side as I raced up the steps to his house. I started pounding on his door.

Come on, come on! Gotta get this shit over with.

Jonesy limped his way to the door. When he saw us through the screen, his eyes went wide. I heard *oh fuck* in his expression before he actually said it.

"Fuck me, guys. I'm really, really sorry. I didn't realize we were doing this thing today."

I pushed my way in and slammed him to the wall. He didn't struggle. I took care not to hurt the stab wound on his side, tender and healing from the melee with the Skulls.

"I know Pop warned you once, brother. Clean up your fucking act. This is unacceptable when we're supposed to use this place if things ever get really fucked up. You understand?"

He shook his head.

"Jones? What's going on?"

My hands started to soften on his shirt the instant I heard the female voice. Fuck.

Lannie came around the corner. She hadn't been at the clubhouse in awhile. Her belly had grown huge with their first child, peeking out underneath the thin white gown she was wearing.

"Sorry, lady. Didn't know you were here."

She paused in mid-step, staring at the three of us. I took my hands off Jones. Nobody deserved to be humiliated in front of his woman, even if he hadn't properly claimed her as an old lady.

"We're just having a discussion," Jonesy offered. "Go back to bed, baby."

Lannie kept staring, her eyes narrowing. She was a homely woman around thirty, but the pregnancy gave her something extra, improving on her looks in that mysterious way only a baby can. She shook her long blond locks.

"I don't think so. Not when these guys come rolling into our house and rough up my husband."

"It's club business," Jonesy said coldly. "Besides, this time I deserved it. We're supposed to clean this shithole up."

"You're calling this place a shithole when I bust my ass around here?" Smoke practically shot out her mouth. "And what the hell's the hurry?"

Bolt's eyes went big next to me. He nudged Jonesy.

"You mean you didn't tell her?"

I had to restrain myself from smacking my forehead. Better yet, his. Dependable Jonesy had really let us down, and that sheepish smile on his face told everything.

"I was gonna do it soon...just as soon as things got more organized."

Fuck. Only one way out of this.

I stepped into their messy living room, putting myself between my brother and his baby momma. I had to be quick and I had to be straight.

"Listen, the club's in trouble with another group. These fucks from a couple states over who've been moving in on our turf. They like to buy off politicians and use women as slaves. I know, it's none of your business, but I'm gonna make it yours."

Lannie's mouth dropped a little. Her lips twitched, like she didn't know what to say.

"We need your house to regroup in case anything goes wrong. I know that's asking a lot, especially after my brother here already took a knife for the club last month. But if we don't have this place, a lot more people are gonna get hurt if the Skulls come around looking for blood. Will you help us out, Lannie?"

She looked at Jonesy. He sucked his lip. Probably hoping she wouldn't put up a fight.

"Alright." Her face tightened. "Whatever! Just keep me the fuck out of it. And don't you dare bring anybody here who'll do us harm with a baby on the way…"

"I promise you that won't happen. That's why we need your house: the Skulls won't come looking for anybody here."

Neither will the authorities and mercs under Mayor Fuckface, I thought. Of course, I didn't tell her that.

Lannie didn't answer. She stomped across the room and headed upstairs, slamming the bedroom door behind her when she reached the top.

"Nothing's going my way today," Jonesy said with a sigh.

I approached slowly, letting him wonder if I was gonna throw a fist all the way until the end. Truthfully, I'd decided to cut him some slack. But this was the last fucking time.

"You've got three days. If I come back and find this place looking like somebody turned over a garbage truck, I will clean this house out myself. Your place needs to look like all the others on the block and stop sticking out like a sore fucking thumb. Got it?"

"Yeah, Throttle. I do." He looked down.

Bolt just shook his head. He was already heading for the door.

"And take some fucking pride in yourself, man," I said, stopping when I heard the screen slam. "I smelled the old booze on your breath the second I got in your face. The Devils are at war, Jonesy. You should know your place as a soldier better than the other guys. Straighten up and fucking act like it."

I was out. We hopped on our bikes and roared out of there.

I couldn't muster the energy to check the garage and backyard like we planned. Didn't need to. I knew they'd be debris fields just like the rest of the house.

Following Bolt back to HQ on the dusty summer road, I kept my radio switched off, preferring the sweet silence.

I thought about Rachel's tight little body. But I thought about Lannie too. She deserved better with a baby coming, even if she was the other half of Jonesy's fuckups. And I was gonna make damned sure that she got it.

A pregnant woman brought out every instinct I had as a man. She'd given him a child, for fuck's sake, the most precious gift a lady can give. Love didn't stop when you claimed an old lady, or just a steady girlfriend-slash-babymaker like Jonesy had.

Whatever Lannie was to him, he'd claimed her in a deeper way. I smiled into the sunlight reflecting on the steel handlebars in front of me.

"Someday, baby girl, I'm gonna take you just like that too." I whispered the words into the warm wind.

Nobody heard them over the growl of the bikes. That prayer wasn't meant for human ears. I wanted to it to go high, straight to whoever the fuck ran things up above.

I wanted fate to throw me a bone. I needed things to settle down so I could possess my girl in the deepest way a man could.

"Hey! Rita, what the fuck?"

I tugged the whore backward by the hair. The animal in me wanted to throw her right through the wall, but club men didn't do that to women.

Even if the bitch had been in my girl's face, menacing her with those stupid long nails.

"We were just…chatting," Rita said, flashing me that empty smile.

I suppressed a growl. I'd never really trusted her, but this really drove it home.

"That true? You okay, Rach?" I turned, still holding the whore by her long hair.

My baby girl's face was flushed angry red. Whatever was going on, it left her shaking, and that made me want to pummel the whore like nothing else.

It really, really did.

"She's right. It was just a chat. Glad you showed up when you did."

"So then, if I let you go, are you gonna be a good girl and go back to your room?" I jerked her hair one more time for emphasis.

The whore squealed. "Sure," she finally said.

"If I see you outside the Purple Room again this evening, I won't be so nice. And don't get any bright ideas about ever riding this dick. It's all going to the girl I've claimed, and that's the way it's gonna stay. Do you fucking job and mind your own business."

"Didn't know you'd claimed an old lady!"

"Not your concern," I growled again. I wasn't going to say it a third time.

Rita swallowed. Hard and flustered. I released her, and her heels clicked loudly on the wooden floor.

"Magus will be in shortly for some pussy. You better be warm and ready for him!" I yelled after her.

Rachel eyed me like I'd gone too far when I turned to her. Okay, maybe I had, but seeing *anybody* menacing my new girl unleashed a special kind of rage. And it wasn't gender friendly either.

"Let's go. My room."

Rachel's eyes widened. My hand was already on her wrist leading her forward before she spoke.

"I'm supposed to finish up with Frannie..."

"She'll understand. We can fill her in later." I lowered my voice. "But first, I'm gonna give you the filling of a fucking lifetime."

That brought a grin to her face. A minute later, we were in my room, the first time her and I had been alone there and about to get busy.

Really fucking busy.

She leaned in for a kiss. Her lips were like candy, hot and sweet, so good I almost forgot what I was gonna say.

"Hey, hold up for a second, baby girl. What the fuck was that really all about?"

She rolled her pretty eyes and tossed her hair.

"Bitch still wants you. So does that other one, the blonde." Extra venom came into her voice when she mentioned Michelle, the whore I'd stupidly let onto my lap the night I took her out riding.

"Did Rita threaten you?"

"Yeah." Rachel pushed her hands against my chest as I snarled.

I had half a mind to turn and break down the door to their seedy little chamber. No, I wouldn't whip her ass bloody like I wanted to, but I'd kick her to the curb. Wouldn't even bother having Pop approve it.

"No, Jack. Don't." Her eyes glowed. "I'm starting to understand what becoming an old lady around here means. Frannie filled me in. If you want me, I can't look weak."

Fuck! The truth hurt like a taking a spill on the road.

"I need to stand up to those whores and defend myself. I know you want to beat them or expel them or something. Let me. Please."

I smiled. The thought of my baby girl turning into a little spitfire was a little exciting. But I couldn't shake the worry that she'd get herself in a scrap she couldn't handle.

"We'll try it. But anytime you go after them, you better let me know, baby. I'll let you do what you need to do. Only if someone else is here to keep you safe in case shit gets out of control."

"Don't worry. I'll break their stupid nails off before they stick 'em through my eyes."

"That's what I want to hear. Right now, I'm more interested in breaking this fucking bed, though."

She squealed with delight as I buried my face in her neck. I pulled her hair, only half as rough as I'd been with skank Rita, tilting her face back so I could have full access to her sensitive skin.

Every inch of her was amazing. I breathed deep and inhaled her scent as my tongue went to work.

She went slack against the wall, already moaning. My hand pushed apart her blouse, showing me her supple cleavage, tweaking one hard nipple on its way up.

Fuck yeah, baby girl. Let it all out for me. I want you to come over and over again.

All for me.

Just teasing her skin had her tensing and whimpering beneath me. Those sounds she was making – I could only take so much!

My free hand darted out, embracing her hard. Secure in my arms, I carried her to the bed and laid her down. I instantly got back to work on those clothes, eager to have her unwrapped in my big old bed.

Her blouse came off, freeing access to the bra underneath. Rach's jeans went down in record time, and I ripped her panties a little when they followed, straight down her gorgeous legs.

"Oh, Jack. Right. Fucking. There!"

Hearing her talk dirty made my cock rage like nothing else. I buried my face between her legs, teasing her clit with my tongue, stopping only to reach lower and shove it up her sweet cunt.

She loved it when I threw that corkscrew twist into my lips. It always drew her swollen nub deep between my teeth, all the better for lashing it in long, relentless strokes.

I paid close attention to her squirming and panting. When she sounded like a runaway train going off its rails, I sucked her clit harder, shifting my face so I could shove two eager fingers inside her.

Oh, fuck. Oh, hell yeah, baby girl.

She was hot and wet and ready. Her sweet puss gushed all over my hands. I knew I'd be tasting her rich cream on my fingers and face for a long, long time.

I couldn't take it anymore. The instant she stopped screaming and settled into a breathless pause, I rose, tearing my shirt off over my head and tossing it behind me.

Rach barely had her eyes open before my jeans and boxers were gone. I gripped my cock in one hand, halfway tempted to jerk it off and shoot my come on her pretty pale skin.

But spending my nut without sinking inside her would've been a crime. I'd gotten her hot, wet, and so fucking ready for *me*, and I wasn't gonna let that sweet pussy go to waste.

Hell no.

I leaned across her and reached for the drawer to my nightstand. Fuck, where were those condoms?

For a second, I hesitated. I knew I could've gotten away with going in her bare with both us on fucking fire like this.

Yeah, in the bedroom I was a wild man, a beast with a growing ache to plant my seed in her womb. But I wasn't reckless either.

Soon, baby girl. Just not today.

I rolled that latex on my cock and yanked her hair. "Turn over and get on all fours for me, baby. Hands on the headboard. I'm gonna watch your beautiful ass shake while you scream my name and grind all over this cock."

"Yes!"

I smiled as she shifted into place. Could this crazy, beautiful thing we had get any more perfect?

My baby girl. My obedient little slut. My *old lady*.

I hadn't laid public claim to her yet with the club, but I think half the guys knew. It was coming, just as soon as we settled this bullshit with the Skulls.

Rachel shifted against me, rubbing her delicate ass cheeks on my rock hard shaft. She knew exactly how to get my attention whenever I let my mind wander, and now I was gonna give it back in spades.

"You need this, baby girl?" I leaned down and whispered into her ear, my breath hot and ragged and ready.

My cock was burning so bad it hurt, but still I wanted to tease her. Playing with her was half the fun. Taking her like a buck in rut was the rest of it.

"Yeah. Yeah!" She whined, a little more desperate the second time. "Fuck me, Jack. I need you in me bad. It hurts!"

Oh, I understood that fucking pain. Satisfied, I latched onto her hips, pressing my fingers into her supple curves as I threw myself forward.

She arched her spine and yowled like a cat when we fused together. I loved it, but I wasn't gonna stop to admire the scenery either.

My hips rolled, thrusting hard and deep, each time throwing a little more energy into my strokes. Fire leaped all the way to my balls and burst up my brain. I watched her writhing, grunting, screaming beneath me, and knowing I was gonna bring her off again just turned that fire into molten white waves.

The old bed hadn't had this kind of assault for awhile. No, make that never.

I'd been rough with my hookups in the past to blow off serious steam. But I hadn't felt anything like I did for the baby girl quivering and groaning beneath me.

I fucked hard to show her how much I loved her, what her sweet body did to me. I wanted every thrust to remind her that she was mine, and only mine *forever.*

She hissed her pleasure, struggling even harder for breath. If I could've seen her face, I would've seen her doing that thing where she sucked at her bottom lip, that criminally cute expression that never failed to set me off.

I knew it. Just like I knew I was gonna burn her down with the next orgasm.

"Come. Come on, baby girl!" I lifted one palm and smacked her ass.

She yelped, jumping deliciously on my cock when the sensation hit her. The heat around my cock increased, telling me how close she was.

Another spank. Another sweet yelp. And a whole hell of a lot more savage thrusts.

One more knee shaking push and she came. I reached for her thighs, lifted her clean off the mattress and hooked her legs to me.

The sudden sensation of coming in mid-air really made her scream. I allowed myself a feral grin, fucking her harder through her spasms, so close to coming myself I could fucking taste it.

Her little ass pushed hard against my pubic tuft. That hot, wet silk wrapped around my cock sucked harder, begging for my come, and I really wanted to give it to her.

"Fucking hell, baby girl. Don't let that sweet puss stop. Keep coming because I'm gonna join you!"

I curled up into her one last time. Cock nestled against her womb, I exploded. Electric heat started in my balls and shot up at once, straight through my shaft.

We twitched together as pure heaven descended over both of us.

Fucking, coming, sweating, rutting. Breathless and beautiful.

I loved her a little more with every spasm tearing through my body, every single ripple I sensed moving beneath her soft flesh.

Coming in unison was pure poetry. I wanted to stay there forever, buried deep inside her, enjoying the heat resonating in our bodies.

Sans the condom, of course. I tugged the used mess off and tossed it in the nearby trash, imagining the day when I'd be home free to go without one at all.

Someday.

"Hey," I whispered softly, settling her beneath me and stroking her hair, bringing her back to consciousness. "You know you're beautiful, right?"

She tilted her head and smiled, answering me with a kiss. We rolled together. I embraced her tight, loving the feel of her skin on my muscular chest.

In this dim light, she looked snow white. The girl could use some sun, but she was beautiful to me all the same, and I was reminded of that even more when I saw her creamy skin contrasting with my dark inks.

Rach lazily ran her fingers over my chest, fingering the devil's head on my breast. "Do you think I can ever have a tattoo?"

I laughed, bent down, and kissed her head.

"Of course you can, baby girl. We'll find something awesome for you after I make the announcement about you being my old lady. How about something that'll be a permanent reminder about that?"

"I'd like that," she said softly.

"Good. Freak's got the skills to take over ink duty, soon as he gets patched in. Man's sure got enough tats himself. I'll talk to him as soon as we've got this other shit under control."

Her hand sauntered down my chest. Lower, lower, a couple inches away from squeezing me between the legs.

Hell, I was already hardening again. Wouldn't be long before I rolled her around and took her on top of me. I loved the way she rode until we both exploded.

"Is everything going okay?"

I tilted her head up gently with my hand, staring into her eyes.

"It's fine, Rach. Our friends from down south will go running like scattered crows on the open road the minute they come here and try to go head to head. We're just waiting for the fucks to make their move."

If she wanted to know about club business, then I wanted to make it crystal fucking clear that this thing with the Skulls would be a bad memory soon.

She relaxed in my arms. Satisfied, she nuzzled into me, and I clasped her that much tighter.

I wasn't lying to her, damn it, even if everything was a little uncertain.

With this angel pinned to my chest, I was determined to beat those bastards back, and make it fucking certain they never returned to Devils' territory.

VII: Anarchy (Rachel)

I was busy doing my first patch up job with Frannie when Tank the Prospect burst in.

Bolt looked up from the table. A hard fall from his bike the other day had landed him in the infirmary. Nothing broken, but plenty of scrapes and bruises.

"Come on! Throttle's ordering everybody to the fall back point. There's been some kind of attack."

"Shit!" Bolt nearly bowled me over in his rush to get up.

The pain in his knees instantly put him in his place. So did Frannie with a gentle shove to the chest.

"You're not going anywhere right now, Mister," she said. "Just because you gave yourself a bunch of sprains and scratches doesn't mean you don't need rest."

"Rest! This is fucking war," he said. Unusually harsh for talking to Warlock's old lady.

Tank came closer, a hulking beast of a man who lived up to his name. If I were new to the club and not madly in love with Jack, he would've been welcome on the eyes any time.

"You heard the lady, brother. We can do this one man short, especially with the boys brought over from the Dickinson charter. Need a few to hold down this place."

"Hold down this place for what?" Bolt winced when Frannie pushed on one knee. "Even those fucking Skulls aren't dumb enough to attack us here. Prez outta have everybody hauling ass after those clowns."

"Don't have all the details." Tank shrugged. "I promise you, I'll make up for it. I'm gonna fight as hard as three men and earn my patch."

Bolt grinned. I smiled too, knowing he was the one man who could literally do what he claimed.

"That's the kinda bloodlust that wins. Okay, hardass. Go get 'em. I'll be here babysitting the ladies since I'm too precious to be doing my job. Besides, I – hey!"

Frannie poured extra alcohol on the nasty scrape he had on one knee. Guess he deserved it.

"Sounds like you're here to protect us. Not babysit," she said coldly. "Rachel, finish up the bandage so we can get this guy out of here."

"Yes, ma'am."

Bolt wasn't the only one who was sore today. Every time I leaned down, I still felt the aftershocks of last night with Jack, the exhaustion he'd left tingling through my body.

We'd been up too late fucking. And it had been worth every single second of lost sleep.

My patient behaved himself as I finished dressing his wounds. Then he was out, heading off toward the bar to mingle with all the fresh faces from the Dickinson charter.

The MC had called in reinforcements from out West as things with the Skulls heated up. I overheard Jack and Warlock talking about Skulls riding through tone in ones and twos, scoping things out, and now it looked like they'd made their move.

How did they know about the backup place? I wondered.

The thought that Dad might've been involved in feeding the rival club information turned my stomach. They'd certainly pissed him off enough to do it. I just hoped rejecting my father wouldn't end up in spilled blood for everyone who'd taken me in.

"How are things going?" Frannie asked while she cleaned up, sterilizing a few metal instruments in the sink.

"Just fine." I looked up. "Jack and I are getting along perfect. He's...going to claim me when all this crap with the other club blows over."

Saying the words was strange. They made me excited, even a little giddy.

Something clattered loud in the sink. Frannie lost her grip, switched the water off, and turned around. She had a big grin plastered to her face.

"My, the boy listened to me. That makes me happy, and even happier for you." She came close to check my work wiping down the table. "Looks good. Make sure that he keeps his word, Rachel. You have to hold him to it, and soon."

"He's going to," I said, total certainty in my voice. "Told me so himself. He's just busy."

She shook her head furiously. "Don't let him pull that delay crap. Look, in this club, there's always something happening. If he really wants to claim you, he'll do it this week. War or no war. There'll never be a perfect time. This is the life."

I smiled nervously. I didn't even know how to pour the heat on him with something like this, but wasn't that a skill old ladies needed?

Frannie reached out and squeezed my gloved hand with hers.

At least I've got a great teacher pointing me the right way, I thought.

My heart leaped with excitement when I heard all the bikes roaring into the garage. That meant the guys were back, and Jack along with them.

I threw down the burn care book I'd been reading and ran out of my room.

I was halfway down the hall when I heard the gunshot. After that, everything seemed to happen at once.

Men screaming, glass shattering, metal and footsteps filling the whole clubhouse with thunder. I froze in my tracks, too scared to move forward, or even rush back to my room.

The door to the meeting room burst open in front of me, and Voodoo stepped out.

"What the fuck's going on?" The old President wore a startled expression.

Another loud blast. I stood like a I was caught in headlights watching him fall to the floor. I thought he'd been shot until he moved, rising slowly off the ground.

He looked my way and his eyes went wide.

"Jesus Christ! Get down on the ground, girl! Down!"

I couldn't force myself to act. It was like all my bones and muscles had locked up.

Voodoo sprang into action, crawling toward me. Catching me by the knees, he threw me down, breaking my fall with his strong arms. They'd probably been just like Jack's when he was younger.

"Stay down here," he growled, drawing his gun. "Don't stick your pretty face up for anything. I'm gonna find out what the fuck's going on here."

Steady gunfire blasted out behind the door. One bullet slammed into the wood, cutting clean thorugh it and showering us in splinters.

Shielding me with his body, Voodoo kicked it aside.

He crouched and fired into the bar, right over the tops of his men's heads. Harsh looking men I'd never seen were everywhere, and I knew by the logos on their jackets that they weren't the strangers from the Dickinson charter.

The Skulls had done the unthinkable. They were swarming in, overwhelming the Devils' skeleton crew at headquarters while Jack and the others had been lured away.

"Stay back!" Voodoo yelled at me.

The President sent out another hail of bullets. A man running across the glass strewn floor screamed and went down. I couldn't tell what side he belonged to.

Several Devils were crawling forward from beneath the overturned tables, Bolt among them. Behind me, the door to the Purple Room creaked open.

Stupid whores. They ought to know better than me to stay put when everything's going crazy out here.

Something jerked at my hair. Before I could scream, I was hauled backward, and dragged through the small opening.

Lilac perfume and burgundy assaulted my senses. I looked up into the Rita's nasty painted face, her nails locked around my neck, so sharp they could cut.

"What the hell do you want?" I coughed. Her grip tightened, and I grabbed onto her gross skinny arm.

I wouldn't be much match for her if nails were the only weapon of choice. But I was ready to get my bitch on if I needed to.

"Just helping your sweet ass to safety. It's dangerous out there, you know." She smiled, blowing the scent of that sickly sweet grape gum in my face.

"Didn't know you'd be concerned."

Heels stomped on the floor from the small bathroom attached to the fuck room. I looked over and saw blondie Michelle. Side by side, I wasn't sure which one looked more trashy.

"Make the little wench comfortable," she said to Rita. "We'll have something to bargain when those barbarian find us. No fucking way am I going to some ratty club down south. Besides, I'm sure daddy would be real happy to have his little girl back."

Michelle smiled. Rita laughed.

I lunged, throwing all my weight into Rita's fake tits. If it worked once before, then it ought to do the trick a second time.

She screamed when I pinched her nipples. I rammed my head straight at her throat.

Had to get down and fight dirty, just like the boys. I wasn't afraid anymore.

Or so I told myself, until Michelle grabbed me by the neck. Something cold and shiny hovered near my skin.

I had to crane my eyes to see the sharp metal glinting near my throat. One swipe with that big hunting knife would've been the end of me.

"Don't move, bitch," she hissed into my ear. "You're our little bargaining chip now."

Just then, the door burst open. Voodoo ran inside and turned, throwing his weight against the door, pressing it shut. More guys were right behind him, and I didn't think they were Devils.

The older man was breathing heavily. He had small cuts on his cheeks and he looked utterly fatigued.

When he finally looked in our direction, his face hardened. "Christ! Can't I catch a fucking break? What's this all about?"

Michelle blinked dumbly. She drew the knife away, moving it to her side.

"Nothing, sir. We were just…"

"Keeping this one in line," Rita finished. "She was hysterical out there. All that screaming would've let them know we're in here."

"Was not!" I yelled.

Voodoo stomped one boot on the ground. His face went bright red and he waved the gun in his hand.

"Everybody shut the fuck up! You whores are in deep shit. I wasn't born yesterday. We'll settle this later. Right now, all three of you just need to zip it before you get us all killed."

Finally. I suppressed a vicious smile as Rita clammed up.

Sweet, sweet speechlessness.

Didn't have much time to savor my little triumph. The shots and pounding were coming close now, and they were nearly right on top of us.

"Who's in there? Fucking open up!" A rough voice outside rang out in between fierce pounding on the door.

"Get over here, you whores. Rita, Michelle, throw your fucking weight into it. Help me!" Voodoo roared, trying to hold back the tide with all his might.

The bitches weren't moving. They sulked on the ground as I got up, stepped past them, and leaned hard on his back.

It helped, but not enough. The door was bouncing open and shut like we were trying to contain a raging thunderstorm behind it.

"Come on! We need everybody to push! What the fuck is wrong with –"

Voodoo toppled backward. I moved out of the way just in time to avoid getting crushed.

Three of the nastiest looking men I'd seen since my capture rushed inside. The big one looked up. I recognized his greasy hair and ugly pot belly instantly.

"Well, well, well," Venom said with a smirk. "Look what the mangy fucking cat dragged in."

All the life drained out of me. I would've preferred to have caught one of those bullets instead.

I was so numb I barely felt him rush forward and crush me up against the wall. All the commotion outside the room had grown to a deafening roar.

Men were still rampaging through the halls, fighting and stabbing and shooting.

I looked over my captor's shoulder and saw Voodoo pinned to the ground by another Skulls member. The man had his boot right on the President's spine, sending horrific force through his screwed up back.

Voodoo screamed. My mind wanted to blank out the abominable sound, but somehow I still heard Venom's disgusting words through the bellow.

"Can't believe my sweet luck, baby. Looks like I'm gonna get a piece of your tight little ass after all. Just hope the shitheads here haven't loosened you up too much."

His hips shifted forward. I had to choke back my nausea when he smashed his disgusting bulge between my legs.

"Try it!" I spat in his face. "I'll claw off your dick if you come any closer."

His eyes flashed. For a second, it looked like he was stunned, but the shock didn't last long. A nasty smile rose on his face.

"Bullshit. You know talk like that just makes this cock harder, right? You might not be a virgin anymore, but I'll tear you apart, bitch. I'll sink it hard and deep and fuck away all the sweet memories you have of this place, just as soon as I –"

"Venom! We gotta go, man. Now! Somebody tipped the rest of these bastards off! The big crew's back! There's too many for us to hold 'em."

He turned away from me, keeping one hand on my throat. I should've taken the chance to kick him right in the nuts. But I didn't.

"Fuck. We can't leave this shithole without a trophy. Alright, here's what we're gonna do." Holding me by the neck, he choked me, spinning me away from the wall.

"Venom, we need to go. Like, now." Another fearsome blast echoed in the hall. "Now!"

The gunfire was closing in, and it sounded like somebody had added a shotgun to the mix. A Skulls guy with a nasty cut along his face came crashing into the room so hard the door broke its hinges. In their corner, the two whores screamed, shielding their eyes.

Venom faced the cowardly duo. Dragging me forward, he replaced the other man's boot on Voodoo's back. He'd stolen my oxygen for too long, and my vision was starting to go blurry.

"There's only room for one little prize on our bikes. I'm gonna let you bitches choose which one I take. Who's it going to be? Your old man here," he paused, jabbing his heel into Venom's spine. "Or this nasty little cunt?"

Stars danced around Rita and Michelle. I needed oxygen. I wondered if I was hallucinating as I saw them look at each other, and then smile slowly.

"Take him," Rita said with a smile. "We know this old dog's more valuable to you anyway. Leave the bitch here. Jack'll never forgive her."

Jesus, no. You can't do this, you lunatics! Jack will kill you.

Venom stared at me sourly, and then threw me down. There was a violent tearing sensation in one ankle, the world spun, and then my head collided with something very hard.

Blackness.

"Wake up, baby girl. Rachel! Do you know who I am?"

My head throbbed the instant I opened my eyes. Overhead, the brightest lamp I'd ever seen scorched down, hot and painful as a sunny day in the Badlands.

"Pupils are responding normally...pulse is good...I think she's gonna be alright."

I recognized the comforting sound of Frannie's voice. She laid one hand on my shoulder and squeezed.

"Jack?" I breathed.

My eyes went wide. I sat up – too soon – and the blinding pain was back.

"Holy shit, take it easy, baby. Doctor's orders." Jack looked at the club's matriarch. "You're gonna be fine. We're both gonna take the very best care of you...and then I'm gonna murder every last one of those assholes who did this. Nobody knocks out my girl and kidnaps my old man. *Nobody*."

Frannie's face tensed. What little color I still had must've gone straight out of me.

They'd really done it. It wasn't just a nightmare.

Shit, shit! I wanted to tell him all about the struggle in the whore's room, the way that one bitch had stood up and turned over their President.

But if she hadn't, I'd be waking up somewhere a hell of a lot worse than Frannie's infirmary. Had that monster with the oversized nails and sour grape gum done me a favor?

"What happened?" I mumbled.

"It was a ruse. Fuckers had one guy come by our fallback point and take potshots at Jonesy's fence. One of our paid dudes in the Cassandra PD said there were a lot more coming. We hauled ass over there. Dug in, waited, and found nothing. That cop fucking lied. And then Bolt called and we found out about the real attack here..." Jack reached for his face and ran one hand over it, stretching his perfect skin. "Damn it, I'm so sorry, baby. I fucked up."

"It's okay," I assured him. Everything was light, and it felt like the pain and drugs were carrying me away.

"Lay your head back down, girl," Frannie cut in. "Relax. I'm going to give you these to help you sleep."

I mumbled something crazy and incoherent. Frannie placed the big pills onto my tongue and tipped a cup up to my lips.

I drank deep and swallowed. Jack never left my side, holding one hand. His smile was big and filled with love, even through the darkness recent events had left on his face.

"Sweet dreams, baby girl. I'm not going anywhere until I need to. I'll be here right when you wake up. I promise."

Blackness. Again.

When I opened my eyes, the fiery drumbeat in my head had settled to a dull ache. I sat up more easily, without feeling like I wanted to gouge my own eyes out.

Jack was as good as his word.

His warm hand was on mine, pulled a couple inches over into the chair where he sat dozing. I noticed the bruise beginning around his right eye.

He'd taken a beating, just like everybody else in that battle.

Jesus, how many weren't even breathing anymore? The thought of any brothers being dead brought a terrible lump to the middle of my throat. I swallowed the bitter sadness, refusing to wake him up.

About a minute later, Bolt staggered in, dragging one leg behind him. I breathed a quiet sigh of relief.

At least that's one more familiar face above ground.

"Aw, shit. I didn't know I'd be interrupting…"

Jack stirred at the sound of Bolt's voice. He looked at me, nodded gently, and then turned to his club brother.

"What's up?"

"Got ourselves an update from Creeper's search party. Him and the Dickinson boys found something."

Jack stiffened. He slid the chair away and let my hand drop. I slowly brought it back to my lap.

"What?"

Bolt looked past him, as if he didn't want to say. My heart began to pound, sending blood I really didn't need into my head. The pain intensified and redness flashed across my vision.

"You'd better come and see it, Throttle." Bolt paused and swallowed loudly. "I'll lead the way."

Bolt turned and headed out of the infirmary without stopping. Jack whipped around, facing me, his face wrinkled with confusion and something else.

Is that fear?

Seeing my rugged lover scared for the first time was like a punch to the gut.

"You wait here and go back to sleep, Rach. I'll send Frannie in to take another look at you." He turned to go.

"Wait!" I screamed, forcing my legs over the table. "I need her now. I want to come with you."

"What? You can't go anywhere!" His whole face darkened.

"I will. Whatever's out there…I want to be with you. I know I'm a not even an old lady yet," I paused, praying I would be one day soon. "But all this shit that went down affects me to. The things that scumbag VP said to me, the way he threatened us…you don't even know."

Jack studied me. It wasn't an outright no, and that brought a tiny prickle of satisfaction to my painful brain.

"We'll just see what Frannie says." He sighed. "Don't know why the hell I'm even considering this. This is club business…"

"Because you need me," I offered, moving closer to him. "You know I'm the one person you can count on right now. I won't meltdown or stab you in the back."

"Yeah, baby girl." He hugged me and planted a quick kiss on my lips. "Just wondering if you know a little too much, too soon. I'll go see about Frannie."

I don't think I ever hugged Jack tighter on the ride outside Cassandra's borders.

A short check up later, and Frannie cleared me to ride with him, to be his support like no one else could. I sensed the fear flowing through him, thickening the entire atmosphere in the broken club with somber tension.

It was an unusually cool summer morning. Peaceful, almost, like the strange calm and dewy softness following a violent storm.

"Right over here," Bolt said over the radio, motioning ahead of us.

A whole crew of the guys from Dickson were parked along the road. I'd seen these guys loitering around the clubhouse before, but this was different.

Instead of chattering, cracking loud jokes, or smoking like normal, nobody was moving. They just stood there like sentinels, solemn faced and huddled against their bikes, staring off across the open prairie, toward the distant hills.

Jack threw himself off the bike and helped me down. I took his hand, squeezing tightly as he walked toward the spot near a ditch where Bolt was standing.

"Show me," Jack ordered.

"Wish I didn't have to, brother. Here he is."

He? Oh, God...

Jack ripped away his hand from mine and started running when the pale, battered shape came into view. His loud, anguished screams exploded in my ears even before I caught up to him.

Voodoo's body was in the ditch, bloody and mutilated. I could only take one shaky look before I had to tear myself away. The savage pain in my head had returned, so fierce I feared I'd pass out.

I saw enough. Jack's father, the former Devil's President, had gaping holes all over.

They'd torn the patches out of his old leather cut and thrown them across his chest, defiling his colors. All his senses were gone too, demolished from his flesh.

Voodoo's eyes, ears, nose, and lips were all missing.

That rock I was supposed to be? Yeah...

I fell to my knees alongside Jack, sending my terrible screams after his, high into the heavens.

VIII: Crystal Clear (Jack)

Pop deserved better. Better than the closed casket funeral we gave him with reps from all six charters in the five state area.

I could hardly believe it when he was hauled to the cemetery in our motorcade and laid into the ground. I never loved my brothers more than when they smacked me on the back, a welcome pain to blunt the tears that came whenever I cracked.

At the big party we threw after – standard MC tradition for a fallen brother – I drank myself into a stupor. Tore the bottle of Jack from Warlock's hands, even when he didn't want to give it to me.

The old man and I had our disagreements. He'd gotten blunt, gray, and way too self-serving with age.

But he was my father, damn it, and I never expected to take the reigns of the Prairie Devils like *this*.

I killed him. Yeah, those fucking Skulls were the ones who took him prisoner and did the dirty deed, but it was my sloppy head-over-heels folly that led us into their trap.

Made me sick just thinking about it.

Then there was Rach. She'd been an angel through the week-long clean up at the clubhouse after Pop's send off. Shame I had to keep my distance.

My head was fucked. Every time I looked at her, I just saw my own failure. She was the last person I loved and trusted who saw him alive, and I still hadn't worked up the balls to ask her what the fuck had happened.

"Are you sure you're up for this, Jack?" Warlock sat at the side of the table, now the oldest active member of this club. "We don't need to do it today if you're not ready."

"I'm ready," I said coldly. "Let's vote."

All eight old surviving members were there, including me, plus two new brothers who'd just earned their patches. Our prospects survived the clash with the Skulls. Tank and Freak had more than earned that CASSANDRA bottom rocker on their cuts below the Devils' face, and the pitchforks on their skin.

I looked at them all. These men were my family now. everybody in Cassandra plus our extended cousins in other charters, now that my last blood link in the world was gone.

One by one, they were behind me, about to make it more official than ever.

Warlock, Bolt, Jonesy, Tank, and Freak. Magus, Shady, Creeper, and Pounce.

Brothers. Family. My blood, even if they didn't share my DNA.

"Everybody in favor of me, Jack Shields, assuming leadership of this club, say 'aye.'"

I watched the chain start at Warlock. Everybody spoke swift and firm, without hesitation, making the whole vote one of the quickest we'd ever taken.

"Anybody opposed, let's hear the 'nays,'" I said.

Silence.

"Congratulations, brother!" Warlock leaned over and gave me a tight hug, pounding me on the back. "You'll make your old man proud. I know you will."

The other guys made fists and pounded the table. When the clatter stopped, I picked up the gavel, slamming it to the wood for order.

The little mallet still felt odd in my hands, ever since I'd begun using it as acting President. But it was more familiar by the day, and now I'd earned it legitimately.

"What's your first order, Prez?" Creeper grinned. He looked menacing and ridiculous at the same time wearing those oversized shades.

"Everybody at this table is smart enough to know. We're gonna give it back to the Raging Skulls as good as they gave it to us. Let's cleanse this town and all the Dakotas. I'm in the mood for a trip to Sioux Falls. How about the rest of you boys?"

Half my brothers showed their wicked smiles. The rest just gave ice cold nods.

"Then it's settled." I slammed the gavel for emphasis. "Warlock, as the new VP, I want you to make sure we're perfectly coordinated with the Dickinson boys. We were good together when the Skulls attacked this clubhouse, but it wasn't perfect. We need to be fluid."

"Will do."

"Bolt, you're Sergeant at Arms now. You need to oversee the armory, and bring everything back here from that stupid fallback point. That fucking thing cost us dearly. I'm done playing defense. From now on, we're going after our enemies. Not waiting for them."

Just like I always wanted. Sorry, Pop. It's not your strategy, but we're gonna use it to kick some ass and avenge your death.

My new Sergeant nodded. He'd be good in real fights, but I needed to make sure he was good handling other elements of defense too.

"Before you do that, there's something else. You're the cleanest looking guy here," I said. He blinked in surprise. "You need to find out where we got that tip about the Skulls attacking Jonesy's place. I have my suspicions. I know our guy in the police wouldn't have turned on us."

"Mayor's office," Jonesy said. "Why do we need to waste our time gathering up evidence?"

"Because it's the right thing to do. There's no more room for mistakes here, brothers. We got fucked up once before on faulty information and little slip ups. Those days are over."

Jonesy shrugged, but he didn't dare challenge me. He was shitting bricks when we pulled up to his house, expecting an attack anytime.

We thought we were smart, that we were setting a trap for those bastards thanks to the tip that came in over the radio. We were absolutely fucking wrong, and I should've seen it coming.

If I hadn't been too distracted getting my dick wet, maybe I would've. Pop might still be alive, sitting at the head of the table and wielding the gavel. Not me.

"Look, I already know Mayor Fuck-face had something to do with this. Probably had his mercs feeding info to the Skulls the whole time and sewing chaos. We just need to make it solid so we're not caught with our pants down again. Everybody good with that?"

I looked up and down the table. Nobody protested. Almost everybody genuinely supported me, and the ones who weren't fully behind me were feeling out the new regime. Now wasn't the time to blink.

"Good. Then let's get our house in order and finish what we started. We've got a lot of fucking work to do."

"My room. Now." The orders I barked echoed in the small infirmary.

Rachel looked up from cleaning. Frannie gave me the evil eye, but nodded her approval at the girl.

Nobody was going to challenge me at this point. Even if I was somewhere between rough around the edges to out-of-fucking-control.

She threw her cloth down on the table and followed me.

"What is it, Jack?" She asked, her eyes big and wide, as soon as I closed the door.

"Sit down on the bed. I need you to tell me exactly what happened that night with Pop. I have a feeling those whores were involved, and I don't want you to protect them. If there's a snake among us, I need to know about it so I can kick their ass out of this club."

She clasped her hands tight on her lap. Rachel looked up, sickly and sad. She hadn't gotten any less beautiful to me, but that face brought pain. Confusion.

Fuck. I don't know what the hell I'm doing here, what I want to do with her.

My cock knew. The beast inside me wanted to throw her down on that bed, rip apart her clothes, and fuck her until everything was good and wholesome again.

But she remained my baby girl. I couldn't do her just to get off like one of the club whores.

"All hell broke lose," she whispered. "I came out of my room, thought it was the club pulling their bikes into the garages. I froze up when I heard all the commotion. Your dad busted out of the meeting room with his gun drawn…"

"Go on. Tell me the rest."

"It was that whore, Rita, who pulled me in their room. I thought they were doing me a favor, trying to get me out of harm's way." Rach's beautiful face wrinkled. "The bitch said she wanted to use me as a bargaining chip. Then the fight spread and Voodoo came in. He tried to hold the Skulls off, and none of those sluts would help him."

I took a deep breath and held it. It was like a stick of dynamite had been loaded in my gut. And the fuse was getting shorter with every fucking word coming out of her pretty mouth.

"I think you know the rest." She swallowed, softening her throat so she wouldn't crack up. "I recognized the Skulls VP, Venom. He was with a few other guys...they held Voodoo down and threatened me. Said they were here to collect a trophy."

She stopped. Damn it, my patience was wearing thin.

"Come on, Rachel. Get to the point. What the fuck did they do?"

She blinked hard. My harsh words were hurting her, and I knew it, but I was like a runaway train at this point.

I had to know what happened to Pop, the naked truth.

"The bitches picked him because they knew you'd be torn up. Rita – God! – she said you'd never forgive me as she pointed at him, hurting on the ground. That slut told them to take him..."

She started blubbering. I managed to throw a lid on the fire screaming inside me. I sank onto the bed next to her and yanked her close, holding her against my chest as she let loose the tears.

"You did nothing wrong. I'm the one who fucked up. I wasn't paying attention before the attack. We all paid for that."

The more I thought about the whores betrayal, the angrier I got. I sat as long as I could, suppressing the killer instinct that would make Rach cringe. But I couldn't hold it in forever.

As soon as she stopped shaking and her sobs grew quieter, I was up and heading for the door.

"Jack!" She yelled after me. "Where are you going?"

"Purple room," I growled back at her. "Those bitches are fucking done."

She ran after me and started tugging on my shoulder as I planted my boot on their door. It was mid-morning and the place was locked.

From late morning through early afternoon, they were alone in there, napping and getting all prettied up to service the boys for another night.

"Open this fucking door before I kick it down!"

My wild motions forced Rachel to lay off me. Several brothers were running down the hall as the newly installed door completely collapsed.

I was in before anybody could grab me. I found them sleeping together in one bed, passed out drunk in low tank tops and matching pink panties.

My nose wrinkled. It smelled like sex – some brother had probably been fucking them both at the same time last night.

"Get up! Both of you!" I growled, grabbing their hair.

Their eyes flipped open. Michelle and Rita did a double take when they saw it was me, manhandling them over to the corner.

"Jack! Whatever you're doing, man, just ease up. Surely these pretty little girls don't deserve to be jerked around like that." Creeper appeared and approached me cautiously, his hands stretched out, like he was trying to tame a wild animal.

"You have no idea. These whores betrayed us all."

"What are you talking about? Just tell us what happened, Prez!" Magus was next to him, tall and wiry as ever. "If there's something they deserve...then we'll vote on the punishment."

I snorted. Fucking democracy.

I'd only been President for a few days and I already felt just like Pop. He'd lived in constant frustration waiting around for crucial votes, especially when we needed action instead.

"They turned Voodoo over to those fucking bastards. That's what happened! Go on, whore, tell them yourself!"

I picked Rita up off the floor. She was shaking, looking up at me, and then past my brothers to Rachel.

"It's true." Rach stepped into the room, taking her place in the middle when my guys cleared a spot for her. "Tell them."

My brothers looked surprised, and suddenly more open to the strange twist. They were willing to doubt me in my blind rage, but nobody believed the baby girl in front of them who nursed their wounds would ever lie.

"Please," Rita whispered, staring up into my eyes.

She was begging. The MC had been her home, and now she faced a dishonorable discharge. I didn't give a fuck that she had no place to go. Bitch was lucky she wasn't getting a bullet in the head.

"Spill it." I nodded once, baring my teeth. "Or else I'll snap those fake fucking nails off one by one. And I should do a lot worse than that for damning my flesh and blood."

I saw her throat twitch as she swallowed. Felt like fucking forever as she slowly craned her head away from me and at the trio in front of her.

"I did it. I had to. The Skulls weren't giving us any choice...they came for Voodoo and the girl here, but they could only take one."

"And you chose him to hurt me, Jack, and this club." Rachel's voice surprised me with its cold certainty.

Neither of us were offering the whore any mercy.

I watched my brothers. Magus' jaw tightened, and he turned away, oddly saddened. Maybe he'd been the one in here sharing them last night. For an older guy, he had a voracious appetite for fucking.

Creeper betrayed nothing. But I had a feeling his eyes were on fire behind those oversized shades perched on his nose.

"Get up!" I yelled.

The whores whimpered as I dragged them to their feet. My brothers didn't do anything as I smashed them up against the walls, both hands poised around their throats.

We don't hurt women. Not seriously, anyway. Not even when they deserve every last thing that's coming to them.

Fucking MC charter. What I wouldn't give to chance that part.

It took every fiber in my body to hold back and live up to the Devils' charter. The club code was painfully clear, and not even the President was above it.

"You sluts are done. Both of you. Have your shit cleared out of here by the end of the day." Tears ran down their faces, smearing their makeup. "And don't think about taking anything that belongs to the club out of this room. If I find out you've hauled off as much as a roll of toilet paper, I'll have my guys track you down, wherever you are. You won't like what happens then."

I released their scrawny necks. I hadn't choked them, just held them in place, but damn if it hadn't been tempting.

"Make sure they clean up this fucking mess," I told my brothers.

"You're the boss," Creeper said. "Sorry I doubted you. This kind of shit...fuck the vote."

I nodded, satisfied, and pushed on. I was halfway down the hall when Rachel came running up to me, racing to catch up.

"You did the right thing," she said. "I was scared to tell you at first...didn't know what you'd do to them. They're total vipers, but they don't deserve to die. This club's seen so much bloodshed..."

"Not my fucking problem anymore. They'll have to advertise their loose pussies somewhere else from now on. It won't be any charter under the Prairie Devils' flag. I'll make sure of that."

Rachel smiled and reached for my hand. That made me stop near the bar's entrance.

"Look, I don't know how to help you with this." She had that big, bright, beautiful stare that commanded all my attention as she spoke. "It's terrible. Worse than anything I could've imagined. I just need you to know I'm here for you...whatever it is you need. Don't push me out, Jack."

I smiled. Her skin was milky, warm, inviting.

I squeezed her hand, leaned down, and landed a kiss on her perfect forehead. I needed that.

Anything to remind me I was still a human being, more than a walking time bomb ready to slaughter everybody who fucking deserved it.

"I won't, baby girl. Just hang tight. I'm gonna sweep this shit away or die trying."

Worry creased her face. She knew I wasn't just speaking rhetorically, and there was nothing she could do to stop it.

"I haven't been here that long, but I don't think this club can handle two dead Presidents in such a short time. You better stay safe, Jack."

"I'll do my best."

One more kiss, and I was gone. For a second, she'd given me that little piece of heaven that seemed lost forever from the time I found Pop's mutilated body.

Maybe if I was wise and strong, one day I'd get it back.

"It's D-Day tomorrow," Warlock said.

I looked at him sharply, more than a little annoyed. Damn it, did he need to give me another reminder?

We'd been frantically getting ready to attack this past week. The bikes reminded me of chariots, lined up side by side in the garages, their steel sparkling like ruthless diamonds in the light.

"You ready for this?" Warlock persisted.

I didn't blame him. Since the vote and the blowout with the whores, I'd thrown myself into logistics shit and kept my distance.

"More than ready," I said. "We're going to kick their asses from here to Kansas City. Did you talk to the Snakes?"

"Yeah. They'll be hitting the Skulls in Duluth tomorrow, along with the Minnesota charter. Further East, they'll be taking out their little outpost in Michigan too. With any luck, the Raging Skulls will be ash everywhere but Chicago and Kansas City by this time tomorrow."

"Good. You did your job, VP."

I stared out the open garage into the big red evening sun. Tomorrow, we were really gonna set the whole Dakota prairie on fire, bathing it in blood.

"How about the girls?" I asked. "We good on closing this place up so that asshole Mayor doesn't try anything while we're gone?"

"Yeah. Bolt said his guys are definitely watching us. The police aren't helping him, though. If anything, they're plenty suspicious of their own boss since he keeps those hired goons around all the time."

I nodded. Warlock flicked a cigarette at the ground and stomped it out.

"I want you to tell Frannie to keep my girl close. Don't let her slip away unattended, even at the hotel in Fargo."

"You got nothing to worry about, Throttle. My old lady treats Rach like she's our own daughter. You know that."

I did. I slapped him on the shoulder before I took off. No matter what happened, I was grateful that I had guys and gals I could count on.

I felt Warlock's eyes following me inside the clubhouse. And I would've been concerned if they weren't.

He was doing exactly what a VP should, making sure the club President didn't make stupid decisions that put people's asses at risk. I'd done enough of that for one lifetime, and I swore it was never happening again.

I hadn't seen much of Rach the last few days.

We'd been prepping like mad for the assault, leaving me little time to take her up on that sweet offer.

Whenever I laid myself down for a couple hours of sleep, I thought about her offer, spoken with love. She wanted to help, but how?

What the hell could she do for me?

That question nagged like a sharp little splinter in my heel. Then the answer came late one night, just after I returned from Jonesy's place.

We were unloading the supplies we'd piled up there when we were expecting an earlier attack. The fallback point hadn't paid off, and now we needed to put that shit to good use elsewhere.

Lannie was there, a little bigger and brighter than I'd seen her before. Wouldn't be long at all until she popped out that baby boy.

At least the stern talking to I'd given him earlier had made him clean up his act. And that made her happier. Jonesy's girl positively glowed as she served us waters and coffees.

Come to think of it, Jonesy himself was a lot lighter too. He moved his skinny ass around, loading up the moving truck faster than guys three times his size. After watching him racing around like his life depended on it, all with a smile, I had to ask.

"What's gotten into you, Jonesy? Never seen you work so hard for the club. Yeah, it's wartime, but is there something else I should know about? You're not using that pure shit we're sending up to Canada, are you?"

Drug abuse was a serious offense in this MC. We made more than half our income on lucrative runs to push coke north and west. But we were strictly delivery boys – never manufacturers who sampled our goods.

He stopped before picking up another ammo box. The dimples in his face pressed deep as he smiled.

"That little chat we had snapped me out of my stupor, Prez. Can't thank you enough. I don't know what the fuck I was doing before…nothing seemed real to me. But after you left that day, I sat down with Lannie and took a good hard look at everything that's mine."

"Not sure I follow."

"Her, the baby, a good clean house…I'm living the dream, Throttle. Yeah, shit's not perfect and there's always some monster breathing down our necks. You know what? It doesn't fucking matter. I've never been happier." He paused, grabbing that box with his skinny hands. "This is dad strength, man. I want my boy to look up to me, and Lannie too. Really puts a spring in a guy's step."

I watched him carry that heavy box up the truck's ramp and come back for another in record time.

Dad strength? I rubbed my chin, trying to get what the hell that was all about.

Later, everything clicked. I smiled so big and dumb a couple guys from Dickinson stared at me until I moved, probably wondering if I'd lost my marbles.

Yeah, dad strength. He's got the best thing worth living for short of this club.

Family.

Just like that, I knew exactly what I needed from Rach. And tonight, I wasn't gonna fucking stop until sunup, loving her the way a warrior should before he goes off to kill.

I was at the bar sipping a whiskey when I saw her come in. Even in those scrubs Frannie had given her, Rachel looked damned sexy.

"Hey! I didn't expect to see you here," she gushed. "You've been so busy…"

"Yeah, it's been rough. I'm taking the night off before the big job tomorrow. Why don't you get all cleaned up and join me? Or do you want to do both at once?"

She flashed that big, hungry smile I loved to see when my words registered in her head. I never knew who reached for whose hand first.

Laughing, we speed walked down the hall, heading for the master bathroom fixed to my room.

"God, I've missed your kisses so fucking much!" The words hissed out her lips when we were inside.

I pushed her against the tiled wall and kissed her neck, smothering her in pure heat. I wanted her – needed her sweet body – just as bad as I always did. Except this was worse, a thousand times hotter and hornier with the mission burning in my brain.

"Throw those scrubs off, baby girl. Time for somebody to give *your* body some special attention."

She moaned softly at my words. I sank lower, helping her push the nurse's outfit off her shoulders, then went to work on her pants.

When she was down to her panties, I started to undress too. I threw my cut onto the counter. Her hands were on my shoulders before I started undoing my shirt.

"Let me help," she whispered.

I stood still and let her do exactly that. Fuck, it felt amazing to have her little hands on my body again. They were so soft and delicate, not yet hardened by all the hard work she was doing with them.

I unclasped my jeans, allowing her to pull them to the floor.

Rach giggled when she caught sight of my cock throbbing through my boxers. It was pressed tight to the fabric, swollen and ready to rampage, but I held it in check.

"Let's go, baby. Shower time."

I helped her up and tugged on her panties, giving her ass a playful spank. I kicked off my boxers, chasing her into the shower.

One twist of the knob and warm steam rained down on us, caressing our skin like sweet peppermint oil. Our bodies collided.

I had her up against the wall again, playfully nudging my length against her soft belly. I ached like hell to slip inside her, raw and forceful.

Soon. That kind of fucking doesn't come quick and easy.

Or maybe it did, but I was sure as hell gonna make it irresistible first. I nipped at her bottom lip, stopping to swallow her sweet gasps.

Her breath and voice sang to me. Each purr vibrating from her throat made me hotter, harder, fuller, and so much fucking hungrier to possess her to the core.

"I love you, baby girl. You know nothing will ever change that."

She opened her mouth to answer, but I sank to her breast first. One hard nipple slipped past my lips and she tensed, crying louder. The bathroom echoed with her pleasure cries, the sweet song that was just an opening act to our flesh melding.

I plumped her other breast while I sucked, loving the way her flesh pulsed against my tongue, a little softer and warmer with every lick.

And those sweet little buds were just the tip. Literally.

I kissed a trail down her wet stomach, urged on by the hot rain on my back. Rach gasped again, knowing what was coming. She braced herself on the wall and planted both her hands on my shoulders.

I licked my lips once and stared up at her. She had to share my hunger, this crazy fucking urge spiking through me.

Fuck.

I couldn't take it anymore. I buried my face between her legs, pushing against her thighs with both hands. I opened her up for the greatest pleasure of her life, running my tongue up through her folds.

Her cream, her scent, I could've buried myself in both for a small eternity. My tongue flicked out, deepening its strokes up her opening.

Each lick reverberated through her body. I enjoyed the aftershocks, never knowing which muscles would jerk in her arms and legs, becoming a little more unraveled as pleasure jolted through her.

Those moans up above became shrill chirps. Her hands moved off my shoulders, wrapped around the back of my head, and squeezed when I started going at her clit.

Fuck yeah, baby girl. Bring me home so I can bring you off.

Scream for me.

"Jack, that feels so good. Don't stop...don't!" One cluck of her tongue stopped her words.

I doubled my circular strokes around her clit, pulling it past my teeth, then holding it bare for my tongue. I smothered her sweet nub in wet heat, winding her up like the prettiest toy I could imagine.

When she came, her thighs convulsed in my hands, shaking along with her screams.

My lips quirked, smiling even as I kept licking her. Tonight, she was all mine, even if it was for the very last time.

Rachel's whole body went slack against the shower wall. My cue to pull away and look up.

"Hold still and kiss me, baby girl." She obeyed like I knew she would.

I kissed her sweet lips as I turned her into the shower. Enjoying the view of her ass while I washed her skin. I soaped her skin up and massaged it, spending extra time on her nipples and between her legs.

I still tasted her sweetness on my tongue. Rach insisted on washing me too.

Turning my back, I let her fingers work all around my Devils' tattoo, scrubbing in deep. Fuck, that felt good.

She swept around me, hugging my whole body, pushing soap and water over my hard abs. And her hands weren't done – not by a long shot.

I lost it a little and tensed when she planted her hands on each muscular thigh. She washed up with her hands, circling closer and closer to my cock. It was raised and pointed like a dangerous arrow, so fucking ready to shoot.

"Ah! Fucking A!" I closed my eyes and bit my tongue when she wrapped one hand around it.

Hardest thing in the world to pry her mischievous little fingers off. I turned around, stifling a smile.

"Don't. Looks like we're all done here. Let's dry off and save it for the bed."

She nodded. I never saw a girl dry herself so fast and run the towel up and down our wet bodies.

Mission accomplished: she was just as eager as I was. Time to spill the beans.

"Listen to me, Rach." She looked up, toweling off my legs. "I've thought long and hard while my brothers and I have been getting ready for payback tomorrow. There's a way you *can* help me."

Surprised, she dropped the towel and stood up, pressing her pretty cheek to my chest. "I knew it. What do you need?"

"I need you to give me what those fucking Skulls stole away from me." I paused, searching for the right words as her eyes locked on mine. "You can help me rebuild the family I've lost, baby. Something to live for, something beautiful to cement our love."

She shook her head softly like she didn't understand.

"A baby, Rachel." I hugged her tighter, moving her up against the wall. "I want to fuck a baby into your sweet womb. Something that belongs to just you and I, our love made whole."

I started to kiss her, needling her neck with my stubble. Fuck, I needed this so much. I needed to breed, to feed my primal instincts firing on every cylinder.

She moaned at first. Then her hands came out. Her breathing was hot, but why the hell was she pushing back against my chest?

"Oh, Jack...wait!"

She pushed. Harder. I threw myself off her and lumbered backward against the sink.

"We can't do it like this! This is way too fast. We haven't even talked about this." Her eyes softened when she saw the flames blow up in mine. "I mean, someday for sure, but this is sudden...I need some time to think about all this. I'm only nineteen years old."

"You're nineteen and beautiful. Shit, look at those hips!" I pointed, starting to get a little flustered. "You're built to breed, baby girl. Better to start early and often. You want to be a mother, don't you?"

My cock ached, swollen and tense as those nipples on her pretty body. I moved forward and tried to kiss her again.

"No, no. I want it when I'm ready. Not like this! This is crazy!" Her dismissal echoed off the walls.

I peeled back, giving her some space. *What the fuck?*

"Look, I don't know what you're going through since those assholes killed your dad. I really *do* want to help you.

I just never imagined you'd want this...it's one hell of a shock!"

"Excuse me for trying to repair all this fucking damage," I said. "If Pop's death taught me anything, it's how short and precious this life really is. We can be snuffed out anytime."

Fuck. That boner of a lifetime was starting to deflate, and my lust was being replaced with pissed off anxiety.

"Pop gave up his fucking life for us." I snorted, unable to hold the anger anymore. "I've turned this club upside down to accommodate you when nobody else wanted to. Damn it, Rachel, you would've been torn up dog meat if it weren't for me and this club!"

"Don't you think I know that!" She screamed, folding her arms to cover herself. "You're out of control, Jack..."

"Maybe that's true," I said. She had a point. "I'm not a very good President if I can't even get my own girl to fuck me. Out of *control* is fucking right."

"It's not that and you know it," she said, opening her eyes. "Being your old lady doesn't mean becoming your slave. And you haven't even made me that yet. If you come back from this battle tomorrow and do what you promised, then we'll see about having a kid together!"

Fuck this! As soon as the words were out of her mouth, I reached to the floor, scrambling for my clothes.

Rachel's face softened. She regretted the words instantly, but I wasn't going to hang around and wait for hollow apologies. Life's too short for regrets, and for all I knew my life was shortening by the second, if fate wanted me to catch a bullet or a knife tomorrow.

I stumbled around the room, clumsily throwing my clothes back on. I grabbed my cut and slung it around my shoulders without looking at her.

Point or no point – and yeah, she had one – I was past giving a shit.

I didn't want this tonight. Not before my brothers and I crashed straight into hell.

If I come back...

Her words stung. Deep. How could she love me if she didn't care if I wound up dead?

"Jack, hold up," she said, coming out of the bathroom a minute later, wrapped in a towel. "I didn't mean to say that..."

Hold up? Is she fucking serious? I've been holding all damned night!

I paused. Forced myself to look at her. If this was really the last time, then I wanted to remember her like the angel she was. I wanted her to remember me like a warrior, not a reckless fuck with real pain shining in my eyes.

"Stay safe and sleep in my bed tonight if you want. I'm fucking out."

She called after me again, but I wasn't hearing it. I slammed the door to my own room and headed for a cot in the storage room, next to the bar where half the Dickinson boys were sleeping.

Fuck it. I'd rather lie with distant cousins tonight, mere mortals, rather than an angel who'd suddenly forsaken me.

IX: Sky High Doubts (Rachel)

The roar of the bikes woke me up the next morning.

I popped out of bed, and nearly tripped in my rush to run to the garages. But the sounds were fading before I'd even gotten my socks on.

Jack and the rest of the club rocketed away without even saying goodbye. I'd slept in his bed, stupidly inhaling his scent as I cried myself to sleep, wondering where right and wrong ended with the insane breakdown we'd had last night.

Later, in Frannie's car on the way to Fargo, I still thought about it.

"What is it, girl? I know something happened between you and Jack." Frannie kept pressing me during the drive.

I wouldn't say anything. I just shrugged, staring off into the dusty summer landscape, sulking through my emotions.

"I'll live. Really, I just want to get this crap over with."

Frannie looked over and raised an eyebrow. "You and me both. Whatever happens out there with the boys today, you'll be on his mind. Count on it."

You can say that again, I thought.

Actually, I was sure Jack would have a lot more on his mind today than our stupid encounter. Seeing his handsome face in my mind made me want to cry and laugh and scream at once.

God, what if something really happened to him? Why did I have to lose my brain-to-mouth filter last night, and spit out the very worst?

Fight or no fight, I'd die inside if he didn't come home safe. I stared at the skeleton crew riding alongside our SUV to guard us. They were mostly older brothers from Dickinson and other charters who wouldn't fare well in the big fight.

Did any of these Devils from afar have old ladies? Did their women survive watching them going off to war and coming back time and time again? Did they give their men families, if only to have a piece of their man to hold onto forever, even if the unthinkable happened?

I closed my eyes and tipped my head against the lukewarm window. My stomach was churning all different kinds of violent, and I'd heave if I didn't stop letting the ride meld with my emotional venom.

"We almost there?" I whispered, turning back to Frannie.

"Yeah, we are. It's a decent place. Business has been good in spite of all the craziness. The club's putting us up at a good hotel." She paused. "Seriously, Rachel. Take some time to relax and look after yourself. There's more to life than boys. Putting love on hold and sorting out the old lady stuff later isn't gonna hurt you. If it's meant to be, it'll happen. Don't you worry."

"What if I don't get a chance to smooth things over?"

She squinted through the sun, studying the worry on my face. Very slowly, Frannie smiled.

"Jack always comes back safe. I've seen Buddy ride into danger and come home more times than I can count. You just get used to it after awhile. These men are tougher than you give them credit for. Count on it."

I blinked at her use of Warlock's real name. It reminded me that he, too, was a real person like Jack, a man who loved the private life with his old lady when club business didn't call.

I smiled. Sage words from a wise old lady.

A few miles outside the city, we pulled in for gas. Frannie shut the ignition, stopping herself before she popped her door.

"Stretch your legs and grab a coffee. It's on me. Just don't go too far."

Coffee sounded nice after a drive that felt longer than it really was. I stepped out into the balmy afternoon, yawned, and stretched.

Frannie stayed behind filling up the truck while our small guard checked their bikes. Half the guys went inside for a bathroom break or smokes. I was almost inside the gas station when something past the window made me stop.

"Holy shit. Isn't that…"

It couldn't be.

My legs moved, pushing me on. The woman who looked way too much like Rita wasn't at the register anymore by the time I made it inside. I stood near the snacks, furiously scanning the whole gas station.

What the fuck? Was I hallucinating? If I wasn't, where had she gone?

I took one look at the man behind the counter. He gave me a confused nod. I just turned and ran, heading behind the corner.

Maybe she'd spotted me and taken off to the restroom.

If there was even a tiny chance of having it out with that whore, I wanted it. If it weren't for her, none of this shit would've happened.

Jack's father would still be breathing, and he wouldn't be freaking me out with insane demands. Slut Rita and Blondie needed to pay, and making them would be so, so sweet.

I rounded the corner and jumped. Rita was standing right there, as if she'd been waiting for me. When she saw me, she smiled, and pulled me into her with those long, vicious nails.

I went nuts. Biting, scratching, anything to break this vile ambush.

Time wasn't on my side. She held on for the few seconds she needed.

I barely heard the van door sliding open next to me. Suddenly, Rita's scrawny arms weren't pinched around me anymore. They'd been replaced by two pairs of burly man hands.

I tried to scream. The man was fast. He covered my mouth with one palm, yanking me into the open black van with his partner.

"Toodles, bitch," Rita called after me with a smile. Then her face went cross. "Hey! Any of you fucks going to give up my money?"

"Follow us to the house," one of them said.

They threw me inside and the van door slammed shut. A man's shoes were underneath me. I kicked, and screamed, but the figure in the seat forced me up by the hair, once more covering my mouth.

"Welcome home, little girl. Did you really think I'd give up after your scruffy little shit of a boyfriend busted my lip?"

Dad's voice. Adrenaline overflowed into my system. I blacked out before I saw his evil smiling face.

"Wake up."

I used to purr at those words, whenever they came from Jack. This time, I jerked awake in my old bed. Tough leather straps held my arms to the bedposts.

Dad hadn't changed a bit in the eternity since I'd been away. He leered over me, pacing up and down my bed like a tiger.

"You've been a very, very bad little bitch. To think, I once felt guilty about turning you over to the Skulls." He sighed in that haughty way that made my blood boil.

"Bastard!" I spat. "Why haven't you turned me over to them? Why am I home?"

He pointed a stiff finger at me, trembling with rage. "Don't. Please don't make me stuff your mouth shut too, honey. I should wash your dirty little tongue with soap and put a muzzle on it. I'm graciously giving you this chance to see if we can have a civilized discussion."

Hate flooded out my eyes as I watched him approach. He sat in the old rocking chair that had always been in my room.

At one time, it supposedly belonged to my mother. I think he left it there as a ghostly reminder, one more sterile artifact usually filled with way-too-clean stuffed animals. My toys, dresser, and neat little desks had always been arranged just so to remind me how alone I was, and how much I needed his all knowing hand.

"I'm going to give you something very special, Rachel." He paused. Disappointment lined his face when I didn't indulge him by asking what. "My admission. I made a mistake with you."

"We're way past fucking mistakes, Dad." I was past surprise with this brute.

"Watch your mouth, you little slut." He flexed his hands on the wooden armrests, bobbing the chair slightly. "Don't be stupid. I'm not apologizing. My mistake was giving you over so carelessly to those gross thugs, but I don't regret it. They wanted to ruin my career."

Oh, what a shame that would be!

I stopped jerking at the restraints. Whatever was going to happen, the bastard had me locked down tight. He was just waiting for his little triumph to sink in, until I turned on the waterworks and melted on my knees.

I vowed that wouldn't happen. I'd been through more in several months than he had in all fifty years on this planet.

I was too hardened now to cry. I had no response for him except grim silence.

"Say something. I need to know you aren't going to fight me."

I shook my head. I wasn't giving this asshole anything. God, I wanted Jack – even if thinking too about him *would* bring on the tears.

"Why are you such an asshole?" I finally asked.

He'd had it. I closed my eyes as he rushed to me, stiffened his palm, and slapped me across the face.

I started laughing, even as the fierce heat blazed on my little cheek.

"That's it? I've had club whores who hit me harder than you, Dad. Too bad it took me almost twenty years to realize what a limp fisted control freak you are."

He shook his head. The rage I saw foaming in his eyes told me he wanted to do a lot more than hit me. But something held him back, and it wasn't love or kindness.

He was devoid of those qualities.

"Whore, yes. That's the right word for you. I know you've probably given some greasy biker scum your sweet virginity, but it's of no consequence."

Curiosity softened my anger just enough to look up. What the hell was he talking about?

"No? I thought that mattered so fucking much to your business partners…"

Another crack across my jaw. This time, much harder than before. Raw heat jumped to my brain as the pain registered.

I jerked my hands, kicked my legs, and smashed his thigh with one knee so hard I was sure he'd bruise.

"Bitch!" He crashed backward, stabilizing himself on the wall.

Guess he regretted not tying down my legs too. Shame I couldn't reach his nuts.

"Stop using that language, Rachel, or I really will gag you. I ought to anyway. You're here to realize you have *no more* say in anything that happens. You're not my daughter anymore. You're my whore to trade away for the best deal I can get. And this time, I'm not being blackmailed."

"Who?" I don't know why the question slipped out. Did it matter?

"The Skulls and I are finished. Whatever dirt they've got on me soon won't matter. Your friends are seeing to that today. The Mayor's Office knows plenty." He gave me that nasty smile, as if I was supposed to be proud of him.

No, Dad. The days of pretending to clap like a pet monkey at your stupid speeches are over.

"A very wealthy businessman from out West has promised to finance my Congressional campaign next year. It's wonderful, Rachel, we'll both be leaving this dingy little town. I'm advancing my career by light years as soon as the voters give me their approval." He shook his head with a smile, relishing his inner narcissist. "You'll be going to my benefactor's private dungeon in Seattle. Tomorrow. As for me, I'll be finding the best condo in Bismarck I can afford, and then DC. Big money goes a long way."

"The Devils are going to kill you," I said softly. "I don't know how or when, but they will. You want my congratulations? Okay, fine. Congratulations on signing your own death warrant."

Dad stared at me for a long time, his eyes narrowed. His fingers twitched. He had to be thinking about choking me, slapping me, or maybe something a lot worse.

He'd always given me looks that were more than fatherly since I hit puberty. I quietly prayed he wasn't even sicker than I thought.

"I thought you might say something stupid like that." Another of his trademark sighs. "It seems I won't be able to convince you how defeated you really are alone."

He turned toward my bedroom door. "Bring her in!"

The door popped open, and one of his mercenaries entered, with Rita behind him. Finally, he'd done something that surprised me.

I never thought he'd let a genuine whore into his perfect home. But there she was, glowering over me, chewing that nasty grape gum.

"Bitch!" Rita spat sickly sweet purple juice all over my face.

One, two, three long jets of grape spit.

I pinched my eyes, ignoring the gross feeling. Too bad I couldn't ignore that stomach churning smell too.

"Skank!" I fired back.

Big mistake. The bitch's hands were on my throat, digging in deep. Her long fingernails really hurt, way more than the pressure from those bony fingers.

"Don't ever call me that again, you cunt. You ruined my fucking gig – my club!" The death grip increased, cutting off my air supply. "It's too late for me and the Devils. But you know what? I want you to remember all the shitty names you called me when you're down on some mattress with your new master, feeling his cigars scorching your tits while he fucks you raw. Remember, little bug, that I did this. I helped squash you."

I coughed. Jesus, I couldn't breathe, my whole field of vision blurred.

"I helped introduce your dear old Dad to his new partner. Knew all about this guy from my old days in the underworld. You think you're hot shit just because you gave a badass MC Prez your cherry. Well, little bitch, you're going to learn all about how depraved and dirty sex can really be with your new owner."

She laughed. Dad stood behind her, watching with glee.

I thought the bitch was going to make me black out. Honestly, it would've been a mercy, but Dad intervened at the last second.

"That's enough," he said coldly. "Our friend wants her shipped off tomorrow. Wouldn't be very nice to give him a girl with claw marks all over her neck."

Rita let go. She showered me with one last stream of spit.

"Aw, come on. Richie likes beat up girls. It's no skin off his back, Mister Mayor," she purred.

"That may be, but I'm sure he likes to...decorate his girls himself." Dad reached into his pants and pulled out his wallet. He fished out at least five Benjamins and pressed them into Rita's sticky, nasty palm.

The whore squealed happily. "Pleasure doing business with you! If there's anything else you ever need…"

"Doubtful. Now, get the hell out of my house."

Rita's stupid smile melted. The mercenary in the hallway came to her and escorted her out.

At least someone else gets to see Mister Hyde. I just wish it wasn't her.

As soon as Dad's mercenary returned, he walked near the headboard and began to untie me. When the second restraint was off, I let my arms fall, neither fighting or wiping the whore's disgusting spit off my face and neck.

"Why? Why are you letting me go?"

"Because I need you to get cleaned up." Dad turned to the merc. "Bring this girl some clean clothes and makeup. Much as I'd like to leave her messy a little while longer, I don't think our client would appreciate that."

I sat up, balling my hands in my lap.

"Rest up, Rachel. You've got a very long flight ahead of you tomorrow morning. My friend Mister Pinkton here will help you clean up." He walked toward the door, but stopped near at the frame. "Take some time to think about what you did. If you'd been a good girl in Med school like I always wanted, maybe things would've gone down differently. You chose this, Rachel. Not me."

The door closed. If it weren't for the grim faced man in the suit staring at me, I would've screamed and screamed until my old window shattered.

Last thing I ever thought I'd be doing after all that went down was taking Dad's advice. Then again, there was nothing else to do but think, not after I wiped away bitch Rita's spit and soothed the red marks she'd left on my neck.

Darkness had fallen outside. The guard dog in the suit now occupied the rocking chair. He'd moved it near the door, toying with his smart phone.

We both knew I wasn't going to make a break for it. Even if I somehow got past him, I wouldn't get past the other guys in the house. There must've been at least half a dozen patrolling every hallway if the voices I overheard through my guard's walkie-talkie were any indication.

And so, I thought.

I thought about Jack. My faith in him and the club hadn't wavered. Our argument last night changed nothing.

He'll come for me. I know he will.
And what then?

That last question echoed in my brain, over and over, a relentless and painful chatterbox. It just wouldn't shut up no matter how hard I tried to make it.

I'd betrayed him.

This house, this hellish life I'd lived before he saved me, was the real reason I couldn't have a baby with him. Maybe never.

How could I make a new life, a family, when the only one I'd ever known was fucked up and sick to the core?

For the first time since arriving at the house, the big wall I'd thrown up crumbled. I paced around the room and sat on the bed, facing the window instead.

The tears were coming, and I was going to make damned sure that asshole guarding the door didn't see anything.

Outside, the clouds had rolled in, smothering the landscape in pitch black Dakota night, dark as the black gold pumped from our soil. I didn't even have the moon and stars to keep me company tonight.

It seemed like the entire world had decided to put me in a box, wrap it up, and tie the string around it monstrously *tight*.

There was a good chance Jack wouldn't find out in time to come for me. Hell, and that was assuming they were winning against the Raging Skulls. Barring a miracle, I'd be on my way to misty Seattle, straight into the arms of another monster who'd do God knows what.

"I can't do this anymore," I whispered.

"Ma'am?" The guard's voice startled me.

"Nothing," I said loudly, annoyed at exposing my vulnerability like that.

Who was I kidding anyway? Yes, life with the club had toughened me up a little. I missed Jack, Frannie, and all the guys who helped show I could be more than a scared little girl.

But deep down inside, that's exactly who I was. This room reminded me of that, and so did the great blackness outside, painfully obvious manifestations of the shadow that had always loomed over my life.

I, Rachel Hargrove, was cursed to suffer. Doubly cursed to realize the inevitable too.

Sinking down on the bed, I thought some more. I thought about how much I missed Jack and Frannie. I thought about how *fucking bad* I wished I could take everything back, if only to leave them with sweet memories when I went away.

Mostly, I just thought about how I was screwed either way. If I wasn't spirited off to a whole new horror tomorrow, then I'd face disappointing Jack and Frannie all over again.

Especially if I went through with my deepest wish. I laughed bitterly when I imagined getting my way, becoming an old lady. If there was anything I was less cut out for...

"Ma'am? It's time for you to wake up."

I hadn't even realized I fell asleep. I sat up, rubbing my eyes, shaking the bodyguard's hand away.

"What is it?" I groaned.

"Your ride to the airport leaves in half an hour."

X: Merciless (Jack)

The sun had climbed high into the sky when we roared into Sioux Falls. It was a convoy of twenty altogether, eighteen bikes and two big vans, all my closest brothers, as well as cousins from other charters.

I gripped my Harley's handles tighter when we fanned out along those South Dakota streets.

Payback was so close I could taste it.

I visualized the Raging Skulls' ratty little clubhouse we'd seen in our intel photos. Those fucks had broken into our home, vandalized our daughters, killed our club's oldest and wisest.

Today, we were gonna bite down on our enemies until bitter, sticky revenge ran down our chins. Today, we were feasting on blood.

Both our MCs were founded by military men who returned to a country where nobody gave a shit. That attitude carried over to our wars, and unlike Uncle Sam's operations, Geneva rules apply here.

Just old fashioned, deeply primal codes of conduct fashioned in blood and steel.

"We're coming up on their HQ now. Got a couple big dogs at the gate." Creeper's voice came over the radio. I'd sent him ahead of our convoy by several blocks to scope things out.

"Deploying sandman dust now."

Fuck, I hoped the drugs in those sausages worked as fast as they were supposed to. We were ready for guys, but the dogs almost threw us for a loop. Having them barking and bringing out the bastards before we were ready – or worse – running around tearing at our legs was a complication we didn't need.

Thank God Warlock suggested the sandman idea before we left. The two bikes ahead of mine turned the corner, and their shithole came into view.

"They're going down!" Creeper yelled. "Everything's all clear for the van."

Off to the sides, I watched the pit bulls go down behind the gates. The big dogs would be out during the whole battle. With any luck, maybe they'd wake up later and mop up what was left of their owners, assuming the Skulls were as big of assholes to those dogs as they were to everybody else.

"Let's go! Bolt, Tank, ram that fucker straight up their ass!" I yelled.

"You got it, Prez."

I pulled my bike to the curb, and the brothers on their bikes behind me followed my lead. The first van sped up, turned the corner, and punched right through the gate with the well worn Raging Skulls logo on it.

Watching the van's back door pop open brought a smile to my face. Our boys with the big guns came running out, and there wasn't even one jackass to confront us yet.

"Go! Go! Go!" Warlock shouted through the radio.

My VP was right behind them, pressing his men on. I watched his frizzy hair and beard bounce as they went straight to the door.

"That's our signal, guys. Come on! Let's get right behind Warlock."

I led the charge, slowing down when I went through the gate to make sure our second van was behind me. I was riding straight toward the big garage, and only swerved away at the last second.

The van didn't stop. Its reinforced bumper smashed right through the flimsy metal doors.

My brothers were in. Over the radio, everybody roared. In the van, Shady and Pounce backed up and pumped the accelerator, crushing the Skulls' bikes inside the garage against the wall.

Those assholes weren't going anywhere now. They were all ours.

Gunfire began to echo in my ears. Warlock and his team had switched on their radios. The din inside their clubhouse made me hop off my bike and move to the service door further back, the auxiliary entrance Warlock and his team hadn't taken.

"Let's go, brothers," I called to my guys. They were right behind me.

I drew my gun. One swift kick felled the door, and we entered, staring down a long hallway winding toward what looked like an area with sleeping rooms.

I kicked open the first door. Creeper was right behind me. The place was so damned dark and smoky he had to pull off those oversized shades, letting his bright blue eyes shine through the darkness.

"What the fuck is this?" A skinny Skulls member looked up from a worn mattress in the first room.

He wasn't alone. I raised my gun and fired carefully over the whore, nailing him right between the eyes on the second shot.

The girl screamed. Who could blame her?

"Shit! Get over there and calm her down," I ordered. "We're way past needing the element of surprise, but we don't need everyone in this area knowing where we are."

I ran into the hall where my other brothers were waiting. They followed my lead, deeper into the complex. The roars of fighting were getting louder, and that told me were about to link up with Warlock's crew.

So far, so good, I thought cautiously, knowing how fast shit like this could turn in the opposite direction.

The hall tapered off in two directions. One on side, the Raging Skulls meeting room. The open door and flipped over tables said the fighting had already moved through there.

On the other, the main bar, with messy boxes of shot up beer and fallen stools littering the ground.

A bullet cracked past my head. I dove underneath the nearby counter, looking up after a couple seconds had passed.

"Go! Flank those fuckers. They've got Warlock and the guys pinned down."

My brothers ran past like troopers. The little niche behind the bar turned into another hall, and I pushed on, straight toward what looked like a big kitchen area.

The place was filthy. Cigarette butts, old bottles, and even a few needles were strewn across on the dirty floor.

I turned my nose up. The Prairie Devils didn't allow that shit. Hell, maybe we'd caught them in mid-piss because half the Skulls were too drugged to fight our ambush.

Whatever. I wasn't going to sneer at anything that made the vengeance strike easier.

The door to the backroom was locked. I pushed, throwing my weight into it. I thought I'd have to peel myself away and kick when it fell open.

I tumbled inside, and barely caught myself by the knees before falling on my ass.

No, not a storage room after all. It looked like a small office, and the big man behind the desk was just as surprised to see me as I was him.

We recognized each other right away. I raised my gun, but Venom was faster.

He got off three shots. One missed, and two hit me square in the chest.

I rocked back, stunned by the bone breaking force. A second later, I was moving forward again.

He was too dumbstruck that I hadn't fallen to fire again. Gave me all the time I needed.

Thank God. Those vests we got from the Canadians on that last run up to International Falls did their thing.

I lunged, leaping across his desk and knocking him out of his chair. I punched the gun out of his hand in our struggled. A couple more twists gave me the leverage I needed to slam the butt of my handgun into his face.

One, two, three big smacks.

He wasn't squirming as much anymore, looking up at me all bloodied, the hatred in his eyes going blind with trauma.

"You fucked up for the last time, asshole. Your club belongs to us now, and we're gonna raze it to the ground."

Venom blubbered, blood and spittle pooling near one corner of his lips. I thought about how I'd seen his face the first time I rescued my baby girl. This sick, twisted fuck beneath me had been holding her prisoner, and then he'd almost done it a second time, choosing my Pop instead.

The animal instinct to kill roared up. I saw bright red, and it had nothing to do with the blood pouring down his face from the spot where I'd ripped open his temple.

"I don't normally take joy in killing anybody, even an asshole who deserves it," I growled, lowering my face to his. "But you're the exception. Get this through your puny skull, bitch boy: you will never, ever hurt my girl again. We're gonna bury every last one of you assholes deep for what you did."

"Wait, wait, wait," he blubbered, raising his hands weakly. "It's war, Throttle. You know that. I killed your Pop."

Fucking monster!

My ears could barely stand this asshole talking, but my fists weren't listening to one more word. I punched him on the opposite side of his face two more times. Only held back because I hadn't quite decided how I wanted to kill him yet.

"Shut the fuck up. You've done unspeakable things to my family, and now I'm going to make sure you and your brothers are finished forever." I lifted the handgun, planting it directly on his forehead. "Quiet, VP. I'm giving you one last chance to take it like a man."

His face twisted. I'd seen it before: grown men tearing up and blubbering like babies when they knew they were about to die.

"No, no…please! I…I've got something you need."

I blinked. Hard. He was *really* testing my patience now.

This asshole couldn't offer me anything. Certainly nothing that would bring back Pop or soften his near rape of the girl I loved more than anything.

I should've ended it then, but my fucking curiosity got the better of me.

"Spill it!" I screamed.

"You kill me, you'll never know what we had on that asshole Mayor." Venom smiled, licking blood off his curled lips. "You want that, right? I'll tell you about it. Everything. Your MC can control that little bitch, just like we tried –"

I fired.

The gunshot filled the entire room, shattering my hearing for an instant. Thick blood spattered in all directions, and it was the first thing I heard pooling behind his blown out head.

Kicking myself upright again, I turned away from his body in disgust.

Shit! Just in time. Another shadowy figure was speed walking toward me. I raised my gun, ready to defense myself.

"Holy shit! It's Creeper, Prez. Don't shoot."

My heart did a full 360 in my chest. I lowered the gun and wiped my face, waving him in.

"What's going on out there?"

"Warlock and the boys are just mopping shit up now. They're all dead. Turns out their President's been dead for a solid month, and this asshole's been filling in without telling anybody." Creeper slipped past me and kicked at Venom's body. "At least, that's what this one Prospect we captured tells us. Only guy whose brains we haven't blown out yet. The rest all went down fighting, or were too high and stupid to surrender."

"Jesus. Any casualties from our MC?"

"Two guys. Snuff and Cerberus from the Dickinson crew." Creeper looked down.

"We'll tap the memorial fund for their families when we get home." Without thinking, my hand covered my President patch, right across my heart.

I didn't really know the men from our sibling charter. Deep inside, I was secretly glad none of my immediate brothers had fallen. Still, it was never pleasant to lose guys, even veteran MC members who knew damned well what kinds of risks these missions carried.

"There's something else you ought to see," Creeper said. "If you'll follow me, Prez..."

He led the way, back toward the row of dingy rooms. All their doors were smashed open and hanging on their hinges. I recognized the place where I'd taken my first kill. The man's blood stained that nasty looking mattress that filled the room, empty of everything else except junk food wrappers and used syringes.

"What a filthy fucking club," I said. "These bastards are in bad shape. Can't believe there was a time when we thought about a truce."

"I know this is gonna piss you off," Creeper warned. "Next room. It gets worse."

Bolt and Magus looked up when we entered. They stepped aside, revealing two crying young girls. One of them was around twenty, and the other couldn't have been a day over fifteen.

"What's this?" I folded my arms, trying to stifle that sinking feeling in my gut.

You already know...

"Found 'em in two of the rooms," Bolt said. "You're looking at the Skulls' prized whores. Two little girls they added this past month, sold to them from somewhere in Indiana. Bastards were gonna add a third soon. You know who."

"Enough." I raised my hand. "Jesus, get them something to eat, and then let's get them out of here. We can drop them off with the police in Fargo."

One of the girls looked up at me, tears in her eyes. Bruises lined her cheeks, the same dark purple hue matching several spots on her skinny arms. She had that dead eyed look I'd seen in junkies before.

I turned away and shook my head. She looked like a younger version of Rach.

My Rachel. Fuck, she's still mine. Nothing about that bullshit between us last night changes anything.

I flexed my hands. Every time I thought about how easily she could've wound up here, beaten and drugged and raped like these poor girls, I wanted to start driving my fists through walls.

Hold tight, baby girl. I'm coming home soon, and we're gonna set all this straight.

Just then, my phone rang. I didn't recognize the hysterical voice on the other end at first. Then a familiar tone cut through the screams.

"Calm down!" I said firmly. "Frannie? Is that you?"

"Jack, it's Rachel. She's gone."

My heart dropped to my stomach like a dead weight, right through my intestines. I braced my hand on the wall, mad blood seething through my veins.

"What?"

"That whore, Rita. We caught her pulling out of the gas station near Fargo with a big van a little ways ahead of her. We followed her to the Mayor's house…"

My lungs died. I just about threw the phone at the wall. But I had to hear the rest of this, no matter how much I wanted it to shatter.

"You didn't…?"

"No, there were too many guards. He's beefed up his security since you rebuffed him at the clubhouse." I heard her sniff back tears. "We couldn't get to her. We waited for the whore, though. A couple guys ran her off the road, found the money that rat had given her. She confirmed everything."

I bit down, grinding my teeth. I should've murdered that trashy bitch in cold blood when I had the chance. The very thought that I'd ever had my dick inside her set fires raging in my head.

"I'll be there as soon as I can. Tell everybody to stay close in case he tries anything else. I want full intel in the next few hours."

"You got it. But wait!" She got me just in time, before I snapped the cheap flip phone shut. "You bring her home safe, Jack. She was real torn up about last night…made her an easy target."

"I'll die before I let her down again."

I started to run and almost knocked down Warlock. He'd stepped outside for a smoke.

"Whoa! What the hell's going on?"

"Talked to your old lady. They've got my Rachel!" His eyes went wide, but I wasn't stopping. I had my eyes on my bike, and I wouldn't – couldn't! – slow down until the road to North Dakota was tearing up my mirrors.

"Holy shit! Let me come with you. Can't let you do this alone, Throttle."

"Then hurry up!" I was already on my bike and starting it up while he was messing around. "Shit, I almost forgot…"

I jerked the bike to a stop next to him. "Go back and tell Creeper to look in that little office where I shot Venom. Tear the fucking place apart until you find anything about Hargrove. He told me had something on Mayor Fuck-face, and I want to know what!"

He nodded, then took off running to the shattered clubhouse, moving amazingly fast for a chubby old guy.

I didn't have time to wait. He'd have to catch up to me on the open road. I wasn't stopping until I was back in Cassandra and had my girl safe in my arms, with the asshole who'd really caused all this dead at my feet.

"Throttle! Are you sure you want to do this by yourself? I can be right there with you in another ten." Warlock's voice crackled over the radio.

He was several miles behind me. At that distance, our little radios started to get hit with static.

"No time, brother. You and your boys can clean up the mess when I'm through with him."

We'd been riding all evening, late into the night. I wouldn't slow down or stop, not even to let my VP and a couple other guys catch up.

My stomach growled. My bones ached from riding and kicking ass all day. My adrenals were totally overloaded, but they stirred every time I thought about the Mayor, torturing my girl by his very sickening presence.

You're dead, rotten meat, asshole.

I imagined his end in a thousand different ways on the six hour drive home. It kept my blood pumping as a late summer evening turned into night, bathing me in those bright prairie stars. They were the very same beautiful stars that showed the night I took her out riding, the night I opened my heart and swallowed hers.

And that made me very, very pissed off.

Letting my crazy urges and emotions come between us last night had been one thing. But letting some other asshole – especially *that* asshole – separate her from me and tarnish our sweet memories was fucking unforgivable.

Growing up, I'd heard Pop talk about bloodlust, the lunatic Kill Everything instinct he'd first seen in Nam. Sometimes, he came home after a big shootout in the club's early days, exhausted and sick to his stomach.

Violent itself didn't bother him. But turning into that unstoppable beast did, after the dust settled and whoever got in the Devils' way laid dead and buried.

Now, I understood.

I rubbed my bloodshot eyes, feeling raw hatred pulsing through them. A distant corner of my soul was a little scared at what I'd become when I burst into that house, praying I wouldn't be crazy and careless. If they didn't outnumber me, I would've pulled off the Kevlar vest to make sure I went into this whole, quick and flawless.

But this wasn't club business. This was deeply personal, do-or-die business, and the die part wasn't an option.

I reluctantly slowed my bike as I drove through town, heading for the better neighborhoods with land around them and neat picket fences. About a block from the Mayor's place, I pulled behind some bushes and hid my bike.

No need to alert those assholes with a roaring engine. If Hargrove was smart, he'd keep several guys stationed outside his house, ready to warn him about the first sign of trouble.

Thick sheets of clouds swept in, blotting out the stars. Darkness, my dearest friend.

I approached the house slowly, taking the binoculars out of my pocket. I hadn't needed them for crushing the Skulls in Sioux Falls, but now they came in handy.

Nobody was patrolling the sidewalks. I sped up, and then really pounded pavement when I saw the sleek black Escalade running in the long driveway. Its taillights flashed red, but it didn't move.

They're waiting for someone...

My insides did another roll when I realized this might be my last chance, my only chance. Of course, the Mayor wasn't going to wait long to get his daughter the hell out of town. He had to move fast while the MC was occupied, when we couldn't descend on him like a sledgehammer.

I crashed behind the nearest bushes, peeping up to look through the vehicle's windows. Didn't see any outlines except the driver.

She had to be inside. And so was Daddy.

I crawled on the ground like a soldier in a trench, quickly rounding the corner leading to the back.

Something was definitely up. The backdoor was unguarded, and I didn't see anyone at the windows.

I'd busted through glass doors a dozen times before, but I couldn't do that here. Instead, I fumbled with the latch, using the butt of my gun to pry the door open.

It popped, loud enough for me to freeze and make sure I hadn't been discovered.

Predictable. These rich assholes were all concerned about looks, not real security in their doors. I pushed the glass door open, gently closed it, and made my way inside.

The first merc I encountered almost smacked right into me. I was rounding a corner toward the long staircase going up, and he was on his way down. I slammed his head into the wall, covering his mouth, and jerked him inside the nearest bathroom.

He only struggled for a couple seconds. One more good skull-bang against the brass towel rack knocked him out. I fished the gun out of his pocket, grabbed his radio, and switched it on.

"Southeast wing reporting. All clear. The dove is ready to fly."

"Bringing her out as soon as we hear from South. Charlie, are you there?"

Dead silence. The guy on the radio repeated the same request. I started to sweat.

"All clear," I said, trying to dull my voice as much as possible. "Ready when you are."

"Roger that. The boss will be making his way down in sixty seconds. He's coming to the airport to for the big sendoff."

Airport? I started trembling with rage.

I knew they'd try to take her away from me. But where the fuck did they think they were going? I had to move.

Pressing my ear to the cool bathroom door, I held it there. Footsteps.

I waited until they were right outside, and then cracked the door as four shadowy figures crept past. Hargrove was surrounded by three goons, all making their way to the main door.

They didn't see me coming from behind. I knocked the rear guard out with a hard blow to the back of the head. The other two spun, guns drawn, but I was faster.

I had the Mayor in a choke-hold his scrawny arms couldn't hope to break. I pushed my gun to his temple. It was damned hard not to pull the fucking trigger and end this shit right there.

"Don't either of you two move a single muscle, or this asshole gets it. I'm not fucking around here. Back off!"

I took several steps backward, going deeper into the house. The mercs looked at each other, and slowly lowered their weapons when I jerked the gun harder into his head. Hargrove's groan was music to my ears.

"Remember me?" I whispered. "I'll wait until your friends are outside. You shouldn't have been such a cheapskate. I know you're not paying your guys enough to put their asses on the line coming after me. You're going to take me to Rachel, or I *will* send a bullet through your rotten brain. With pleasure," I added.

I was breathing fire in his ear. He trembled in my arms, making tiny sounds like a whiny kid.

"Please...please don't. Anything you want. It's yours."

Is it really that easy?

I jerked him backward, dragging him upstairs. The two men waited near the main door leading to the long driveway. When they didn't open it and go out, I fired at the chandelier above them.

One man screamed as glass rained down around them, grazing that neat suit, and probably some skin. They turned and ran out the door before I could get off a second shot.

"Rachel's room, or wherever the fuck you're holding her. Right now."

The Mayor marched on. Warlock was only a couple minutes behind, and he had the firepower from the fight with the Skulls to pin down all three mercs by the vehicle outside. I just wanted to do what I had to do before any of my brothers joined me in the house.

"Here?" We'd stopped in front of a door.

Hargrove nodded. "I gave you what you wanted…can't we back off this? Just a little?"

I stared at him, resisting the urge to plant a bullet in his spine at the spot where I now had the gun against him.

"No, we can't. Last time I let you slip away with a slap on the face, you tipped off a rival MC and killed my father. You blew the second chance you never deserved, and I'm not making that fucking mistake again. Get in there!"

I stabbed the gun into his back. Hargrove jumped forward. He popped the exterior-only lock to the room and we were in. Behind another guard, I saw Rachel, and the man began reaching for his gun.

"Don't. I won't hesitate to kill this asshole. Believe me, it's rough just keeping him hostage. Go join your boys downstairs."

The merc dug his feet into the ground and stared at me for several seconds. For a moment, I thought he was going to try something stupid, and then I'd have to fire – hopefully faster then him.

The death glare I always gave my enemies never failed.

He began to back off, lowering the gun to the floor. I let him slip slowly past me. I kept my gun trained on him over Hargrove's shoulder as he disappeared down the hallway.

Stepping back into the room, I kicked the door shut and lowered my weapon, holding one arm around the asshole. Rachel was on me in a heartbeat, falling into the embrace I offered with my free arm.

It was like a weird family group hug. On one side, the woman I loved most. On the other, her own flesh and blood, the man who'd tormented her, who deserved a special kind of death.

"I knew you'd come," she purred, then turned back to the Mayor. "And I promised you he would, Dad. You should've hopped on that plane yourself and let me go. Now, it's too late."

"Get on the bed, asshole!" I shoved my knees into the backs of his, knocking him flat on the floor.

Hargrove grunted, staggered up, and crawled to the bed. When he was sitting up and looking at us with his dark eyes, I passed the gun into her tiny hands.

"This is all you, baby girl. You should be the one to put a bullet between his sick eyes. Just say the word and I'll give you the space to do it."

Her pupils shimmered like black pools when she looked at me, as if she couldn't believe what was happening. My girl knew me as the adjudicator of life and death, but this time, I was handing that power over to the one who deserved it most.

"Are you sure?" She asked, staring at me, and then taking a good, long look at her father. "If there were another way...I'd make him live in his own hell. A bullet seems too easy."

"It is," I said. "But I think we both know every second this asshole is still breathing means more problems down the line for us."

"Will you two just get on with it?" The Mayor sneered, craning his face up.

Rachel turned toward him again. This time, all her uncertainty was gone, smothered the instant she heard his wicked, condescending tone.

"Do it, Rach. I'm right here with you."

I smiled as she raised the gun. I squeezed her shoulder and let my hand drop, giving her the space she needed.

Just then, the door blew open. I spun, ready to send my fists flying into any guards who'd been stupid enough to try to rescue their master. I almost punched my VP instead.

"Hold it! Jesus, just a second, Throttle. There's something you should hear. Her too!" Warlock pointed past me at Rachel.

Shocked, she lowered her shaking hands. I gritted my teeth. Nothing worse than having the energy sucked out of you right when it matters most.

"This better be good."

"Creeper got me that intel he found in Venom's office down in Sioux Falls. You're gonna want to hear this…"

I leaned in reluctantly. Warlock's big bushy beard tickled my ear as he whispered. I locked eyes with Rachel, and she watched me, wondering what he was saying.

"Okay, okay." I sighed. "Give me that gun, baby girl. Believe it or not, there's a better way to deal with him."

"Huh?" She stepped back, a little closer to the Mayor than I liked, her face tense.

"It's okay. If you don't like what I offer, I'll hand it right back to you and we can finish what we started." I looked at Warlock and disappointment lined his old face.

Too bad. This was her decision.

"Come on. Just let me make the pitch."

"Fine," she said, jerking the gun toward me.

Rachel was irritated with the back and forth bullshit. I didn't blame her. I waited until she was right next to me before lifting the gun at the red faced monster sitting on the bed.

"Okay, asshole. This is how it's going to go. From now on, you're going to be looked after by my club. Surrounded, twenty-four-seven. Your office, your home, anywhere you go. The Prairie Devils are gonna be your second shadow. You'll serve us even more faithfully than that bullshit office you claim to serve, and you'll never move up the ranks. You're our Mayor now, and you have no second choices."

He chuckled nervously. "You're really serious, aren't you? And just why the hell would I agree to this crap?"

"Because if you don't, it'll be a big con slitting your throat one dark night in a prison cell, rather than your own daughter sending hot lead through your skull."

His face went white. "You...you know."

"Yeah, I do. The shit in that report is enough to get you a death sentence if it were up to the MC or anybody else with a strict sense of justice. Most criminals don't take too kindly to scummy politicians who make their money off children."

Rachel stepped forward, eyes like needles aimed at her father. "What's he talking about?"

Hargrove shook his head. I never thought the bastard would show any sense of shame. But he did.

He refused to answer her. I came up behind her, gently squeezing one shoulder.

"If you're not gonna say it, then I will." I looked at Rachel. There was no easy way to deliver this news. "You're not the only woman this asshole's tried to sell off to advance his career. Just the oldest and most closely related. The Raging Skulls were blackmailing him because they hired a PI to dig into our friend here. Turns out that big fortune he funneled through the old business for campaign contributions originated in child trafficking."

"Oh my God..." Rachel sputtered, and her face reddened.

Hargrove coughed, shifting uncomfortably. I couldn't take this shit anymore. I lunged forward, grabbing him by the neck. I intended to slowly choke him just to the point of passing out.

"Your dad goes a long way back with some serious criminal organizations. He likes to pretend he's miles above them, but we know the truth. Don't we, Mayor?" His hands wrapped around mine, desperately struggling to pry my fingers off him as I bent them into his neck. "Doesn't surprise me that he's tried to worm his way up in politics, where all the big crime bosses go."

"Throttle…" Warlock looked at me, concern raging in his eyes.

"How 'bout it, Rach? I know you want to finish the job, just like me, but my VP here says there's a better way. We can keep this asshole under our control, never out of sight, and make sure he never hurts anybody again. The Skulls did a shitty job of blackmailing him because they were high and disorganized." Baring my teeth, I leaned forward, until I was face to face with the Mayor. "That's not the case with our MC. We know how to use incriminating evidence the right way. And we will."

I had to release him. He fell back, coughing, struggling for air.

"Well?" I turned to Rachel.

She looked at me for nearly a minute, thinking hard. "Okay. I like your way better. A quick shot to the head sounds too easy for him. This…it'll make him suffer."

I nodded. So did Warlock, clearly relieved we were doing the smart thing. Not to mention the safe thing – killing Cassandra's Mayor would've invited more problems covering it up.

"Can you hear me, Mayor? I'm going to tell you exactly how it's going to go since your daughter's kindly decided to spare your shitty life. Answer me!" I grabbed his short hair and jerked.

Finally, he nodded. His throat was too damaged to speak.

"No more goons. You're going to let these men off your payrolls tonight. If we find out you try to bring in more bodyguards or pull one over on us in any way, then I won't hesitate another second to finish off what Rach and I started tonight. Understand?"

"Y-yes. I...understand."

Rachel looked away in disgust. I twisted his head one more time, pulling him close. I wanted to see the terror in his eyes.

"From now on, the Prairie Devils are gonna be your permanent security detail in this town. Not to protect your ass, but to keep the rest of the world safe from you, and any of your fucked up associates. You'll pay us well too. No salaries. That filthy money's gonna get donated bit by bit to the charity of our choice, until it's all gone or you lose your next campaign."

I shoved him back on the bed, grabbed Rachel by the hand, and stopped near the door to talk to Warlock. "Get a couple guys down here right now. This asshole's all seeing eye starts now."

"You got it." My VP smiled. I could tell he was enjoying this.

Having a puppet in the Mayor's office promised to bring a lot of good to the club. Shame it meant I had to reassure Rachel, and myself, that we'd done the right thing.

The front door was ajar. I opened it carefully, and instantly noticed the Escalade in the driveway was empty.

The little black car parked next to it was gone too. The mercs had fled, all except the one I knocked out in the bathroom. I'd make sure they got some small hazard pay in return for keeping this shit quiet.

Soon, we were out in the surprisingly cool night. I held Rachel's hand, preventing her from climbing on my bike like she wanted.

"What?"

"He's never gonna hurt you again, baby girl. Nobody ever will. All that shit that went down between us yesterday...I screwed up. Pop's death messed up my mind. Now that his ghost is satisfied with blood, I'll lick my wounds and regain my senses. I'm sorry." I looked at her without blinking.

"So am I," she said softly. "I shouldn't have been so harsh...the whole time he had me here, all I could think about was you, how the last thing I said might be you thinking I didn't want you to come home safe."

Her lips twitched. Before she started to cry, I tugged her forward, embracing her tightly over my bike. Damn, I wish we didn't have that machine between us just then.

"Don't you worry about that. Crazy shit brings out a lot of emotions. Truth is, I'm in this for the long haul, and you're gonna be my old lady this week. I promise." I looked away, loving the way the overhead stars reflected in her loving eyes.

The skies were clear again. If I were a deeper man, I would've wondered if it was a sign. But the only sign I needed was her sweet smile.

"I'm keeping my word, no matter what happens. Doesn't matter if you want to make a family with me next sunrise or next decade. I love you, Rach, more than I ever thought I could love a woman. Life in this club always has its worries, but I'm never gonna let them get between us again. That means my own bullshit too. You're too important for that, and so is this thing we have."

"I love you too," she whimpered, shedding a couple tears. Mostly, she was just smiling.

I held her tight, rocking her gently beneath the high night sky. Even when more brothers pulled up from the club and walked past us, I didn't let go. They'd better get used to it. Everybody was gonna know about us soon.

When she peeled away from me, I rubbed my arm into the spot where her tears had fallen. They christened several patches on my jacket, and I wanted them to. I wanted her tears to stain deep, to make me remember this night forever.

"Hold on tight, baby girl. Let's go home."

XI: New Blood (Rachel)

Jack kept his promise. It took a few days to organize the big party for the guys, including the Dickinson charter who'd done so much to cleanup everything.

I wanted to help with the prep work, but Frannie wouldn't let me do anything. She just made me rest. I listened reluctantly. I knew it would help soothe the guilt she still felt over my capture.

The big night came. The club guys set up some grills in the big fenced in lot attached to the clubhouse.

Smokey meats of all kinds filled the air, melding with generous liquor into a spicy perfume. I never thought I'd love a smell like that. But I did.

Night wore on, and the bonfires roared high into the darkness. I sat near the head of the big table with Jack, sharing a huge steak he cut into pieces for me. I stole his glances and his smiles, all damned sexy, in between bites.

"You ready for this, baby? I think it's time, before everybody's too drunk off their asses to look at me straight."

I laughed and nodded. God, I shouldn't have been the one so crazy nervous. He was going to be speaking in front of all these gruff men, old ladies, girlfriends, and kids, after all.

But I think I forgot how to breathe as Jack stood up, climbing onto the table and waving his arms. "Everybody listen up! I've got an announcement I want the whole club to hear. Dickinson too! You boys can send it out to all the charters."

That got their attention. Too many eyes to count focused on their President. Intensity ruled.

"I appreciate the full measure every brother's thrown into this fight the last few weeks. In case anybody wondered about the change in leadership: don't. We've proven the Devils are gonna continue knocking down every last MC who rises up to get in our fucking way."

"You tell 'em, Prez!" A voice roared.

"I will. And I'm also gonna tell you all how grateful I am to someone who isn't a brother, but is part of this MC. I'm really standing here tonight to tell you all about my new old lady."

He paused. Several gasps rose from the crowd – mostly women – instantly followed by a few bawdy whistles.

"Stand up, Rach." He stared at me, and I did as he asked, gulping the whole time. Jack took my hand. "Most of you know Rachel as your nurse and Frannie's right hand girl. Well, now the best old lady in the Cassandra charter's finally got an equal. I'm claiming this sweet, caring, intelligent girl as mine tonight, and only mine. And if anybody in this MC wants to give her shit or challenge that, then my fists are ready."

Quiet. Then the loudest, wildest round of applause, hoots, and hollers I'd ever heard broke out.

Jack jumped down off the table and hugged me tight. Would I ever stop staining his leather cut, crying all over him?

Maybe one day, if this beautiful man stopped overwhelming me. But I couldn't imagine when that would happen.

"I love you, Jack," I whispered in his ear. "Thank you so, *so* much."

"Congratulations, baby girl. You're one with me and my club now. There's no going back from this. Once you're in this MC, you're here forever, and that goes for more than just full patch brothers."

The men were already making the rounds. Warlock and Frannie were the first to come over, patting him on the back.

"I knew you'd get around to this one day. I could tell by the way you looked at her since we picked her up. She's gonna look gorgeous in tats."

Jack broke our embrace to give his VP a big bear hug. Without even waiting for me to step forward, Frannie hauled me into her arms, planting a big kiss on my cheek.

"Congratulations, hon. We're all real family now. Just don't let big daddy walk all over you," she whispered.

Good advice. As always.

A couple seconds later, and the old couple were pushed aside by more eager friends. Men and their families kept going like a long wedding reception line, shaking our hands and slamming Jack on the shoulders. If they weren't sore by the end of the night, I'd be amazed.

"Hey, what was that Warlock said about tats?" I asked, just as the crowd was tapering off to go back to their booze and ribs.

"As my old lady, you get the official seal. Come on. I know just the man to see."

With as many tattoos as Freak had, I didn't have any doubt he'd do a good job. I held Jack's hand the whole time as he laid me down on the padded bench in the garage, a full set of inks in front of us.

"You want the standard old lady stuff or should I make it extra pretty?" Freak asked.

"Let's make it a small pitchfork, just above the wrist for the MC. For me, all I want are the words, fancy as you can make 'em. Property of Throttle, Prairie Devils, Cassandra. Is that all good for you, baby girl?" Jack smiled, a big wild grin surrounded by lips I wanted to get lost in.

"Yes!" I didn't even hesitate.

Freak went to work, pointing the needle gun at my virgin flesh. It wasn't as painful as I expected.

Over the next hour, I watched each letter come into view, glancing up at Jack and barely suppressing my giddy excitement as his brother engraved my arm.

I studied the sweet flourishes. Just like he said, it was tasteful, but bold. Like something you'd see on a fine bottle of bourbon – strength and elegance balanced together.

Just like him and I, I thought, looking up into Jack's gorgeous face again.

When it was almost over, he leaned in and laid a quick kiss on my forehead. I didn't need to read minds to know he wanted to get out of here as badly as I did. He'd given me both my special surprises tonight.

Now, I had one for him, and I was aching to turn it over.

"Are we finished?" I looked up at Freak after he pulled the needle gun away.

"You're all good to go. I'd let that shit settle and follow the after-care instructions on this sheet." He pushed a piece of paper toward me, and then Jack tore it out of his hands.

"I'll take care of her, man. Not like I haven't gotten these myself a dozen times before. We've still got a long night ahead of us."

Freak nodded, rolling his shoulders in submission to the President. "You're the boss. Between that speech and what I just slapped on her arm, everybody knows she's yours now."

"Damned right." Jack held out his arm to help me up.

He allowed a thin smile to line his lips. When I was on my feet again, he pulled me in close, wrapping his arms around me and kissing me in plain view of his heavily tattooed subordinate. His hands swept down my lower spine, spread along my ass cheeks, and cupped them through my jeans.

I purred, pouring honey sweet heat into his mouth, opening for his tongue.

God! I think he knows it, before I've even said anything...

Heat pulsed through me, winding through my core. I was shocked, a little embarrassed, but mostly just hot as all hell.

"Let's get going, baby. My room."

Jack never eased up on holding my hand. He pulled me forward, shooting Freak a defiant look on the way out. The new member held his tongue and gawked, amused beneath all his ink and piercings.

We headed straight for his room. It was remarkably quiet inside the clubhouse with almost everybody else outside. The Purple Room remained vacant, though Frannie told me they were looking at some new girls to usher in next week.

"Will I get a chance to make sure the newbies aren't assholes?" I said.

Overcome by lust, Jack stopped and needed a second to realize what I was talking about. Then he motioned toward the whores' room and nodded.

"You'd better. This club can't stand anymore backstabbing bitches around here. You're gonna be screening the girls with Frannie for all the standard health shit next week. Interrogate to your heart's content." That made me smile. "If anything puts you off, make sure I know about it."

"You will."

Jack wasn't having anymore delays. His hot, rough arm tightened around my wrist, jerking me into his room and slamming the door behind him with a quick jerk.

It felt like I'd been away from this bed for an eternity.

I collided with him instantly, flattening myself against his chest, digging my nails into his sweet bulk. I needed this, needed him to hold me, hot and bare, the kind of grip that said *forever*.

He cupped my ass again, harder now that we were alone. He squeezed my tender flesh in sharp, steady strokes, all the while circling his unstoppable tongue across my lips, reaching for mine.

I melted into him.

With this man, everything came natural, even if my sexual experience hadn't evolved much beyond a virgin's.

Not yet. But all that was about to change.

I raked my nails softly over his leather and began dropping to my knees. His eyebrows quirked in surprise when I went right for his fly, opening the zipper and searching for his cock.

It sprang out, straight into one hand. I pumped it several times, pausing my lips just over its surface to bathe it in hot steam.

"Fuck!" Jack growled. "Where the hell did you learn to tease like that, baby girl?"

I answered him by narrowing my tongue and running it along his base, gently massaging his balls in one hand.

He tasted good. Raw, earthy, masculine good.

I was horny for his touch before, but now nothing short of a nuclear blast was going to stop me. I tilted my head, applying one long wet kiss to the underside of his erection, flicking my tongue against his beautiful length on the way up to the head.

"Fuck! Nobody does it for me like you…"

More rough music to my ears rained down on me when I finally drew his tip into my mouth. I sucked low, sucked deep, urging him to push his fingers through my hair with little twists of my head.

It gave a nice corkscrew motion to my efforts as I went down. I had a lot to learn about giving head, but I already knew men liked it hard. I gave it to him just like he wanted, pursing my lips as tight as they would go.

Up and down, up and down. Jack's pressure on my head increased, and he yanked at my hair a little more for support each time I completed a new circuit.

"Yeah, those tight little lips look perfect wrapped around my cock. So does that new stamp." My arm was twisted in a way where he could see *Property of Throttle* newly engraved on it.

The fire inside me rose. I worked even harder, shifting my thighs together to contain the inferno.

His body tensed a little more with every stroke. Part of me wanted to bring him off in my mouth, but I couldn't do that, not yet...

"What? Why'd you stop, baby?" Jack opened his eyes and looked down at me.

I wiped my mouth. "I need your seed for something else."

Grabbing his stiff forearms, I helped myself up, rubbing my body on his. I kissed a long line up his neck, waiting until I reached his ear to speak.

"I've thought about the other night, and I changed my mind. Things are different now, Jack. I'm your old lady – your property." His breath hitched when I said it, and I smiled. "Give me a baby. If I'm going to be claimed by you, I want to go all the way. Own me forever."

When I peeled away and looked into his eyes, they burned brighter than before. Hell, bright was an understatement.

His beautiful eyes were positively glowing. He seized my wrists and pulled me close, breathing hot breath on my lips, less than an inch from devouring me in new kisses.

"This isn't a crazy tease? You're serious?"

"Would I lie to you?" I cooed, flicking my soft tongue against his firm lips. "That's a tease. What I just told you isn't."

Growling, he lifted me off my feet and threw me over his shoulder. He stomped quickly to the bed and tossed me down on his mattress, landing on top of me.

His hands had never moved so fast to tear away our clothes. I helped him work off mine, and then his, until we were naked. Our bodies instinctively knew what was about to happen, and they were running all over themselves to fulfill that mating ache, that breeding fire.

Jack lifted my arms high above my head and pinned my wrists with his. He shifted forward, pushing his bare cock against my slit. I moaned loud, right into his ear, pumping my hips up.

His length fit wonderfully between my lips, hot and sweet and hard as warm stone. But I didn't want him between my weeping labia – I wanted him inside me.

"Now who's teasing?" I whimpered. Again he rubbed his swollen head on my clit, oiling his shaft in my cream.

"You're right. I think we've had enough play, baby girl. I just wonder who wants some real hard fuckin' worse. You, or me?" Smiling, he bent his head, scraping my cleavage with his stubble and taking my right nipple into his mouth.

He bit down, squeezing the sensitive bud. Pleasure exploded in my brain, so fierce I could barely speak.

My hips gyrated, grinding against him, working his cock up and down with my softness. God, he needed to give in and fuck me, and he needed to *now*.

Jack tilted his hips, repositioning his cock. In one jerk, he slammed forward, pushing up into me. Deep, hard, and so fucking hot.

I lost it.

I came instantly. Gushing, screaming, and convulsing all over him. My womb twitched, sending its shocks through all my muscles, sucking at the hard spike he held inside me, hard and unmoving.

Shuddering beneath him, he kept his head near my breasts, plucking at my nipples. My legs curled around him, and I'd barely finished coming as he began to thrust.

"That was quick, Rach. Fast, but beautiful. No worries. We're gonna make it happen again before I fill you up."

"Yes! Yes!" I gurgled the word over and over, too drunk on hot ecstasy to say anything else.

Having him deep inside me every time before was downright exquisite. But I didn't have a clue how different going bare could be.

His length slid perfectly through my wet silk, just like nature intended. It was divine, total carnal perfection in every stroke.

I felt each layer in his movement when he thrust deep, stopping only to make sure I was still pinned down. My hips bucked back, swallowing his cock, lifting my body a little higher when my legs pulled on his.

"That's it, baby girl. Grind your pretty clit into me."

Yes! I couldn't even say it anymore.

I just thought it, pushing up into him, loving the way his balls slapped against the soft curve underneath my ass. And he was fucking harder all the time, burying himself to the hilt.

Soon, he pinned me into the mattress, entangling me deeper in his thrusts. I only lifted up when he did, slamming hard against the squealing bed springs.

The fire that rushed through me before became ten times hotter. I wondered if I'd come without passing out the next time I spasmed, and that sweet surrender was coming fast.

"Come with me, Jack," I panted out. "Give me your beautiful baby. I want a family with you."

"Oh, fuck. Fuck. Fuck!"

Three times, he cursed, each one a little sexier than the last.

I knew he was getting close. I clenched everything beneath my waist, from the velvet wrapped around his cock to my legs moving with his like welded pistons.

Give it up, lover. Give me our baby. Give me part of your soul!

His grip on my wrists coiled so tight it hurt. The sharp bite was just the overload I needed, sending me spiraling into another explosive climax.

I screamed, trying to cry out his name, but failing. I wanted anybody in earshot through the walls to know who was owning me like this, who'd tamed my virgin flesh, and now my ripe little womb.

Then there was an explosion above me like thunder. I looked up through the blurry heat filling my eyes and saw him jerk, felt him turn to granite everywhere we touched.

Jack stabbed forward and gave me what I'd been pleading for.

His come shot deep. It burned like pure fire, racing up into me, lapping against my walls.

Jack grunted above me, his guttural pleasure timed to his spasms. I came even harder, drawing his seed into me, wishing we could stay locked together this way forever.

The raging fire exploded through my whole body, and then edged back. The fireball lost its wild temper and sizzled lower, into a pleasing afterglow. Our bodies stopped twitching and he collapsed on his forearms, holding himself over me.

I sighed softly. He remained buried in me, even as he touched his forehead to mine.

"Fucking incredible. Did you ever imagine it would be that good?"

Hell no! I shook my head.

What really amazed me was that he sounded just as surprised as I was. It warmed my heart to know my flesh brought him such pleasure, making an older, experienced man feel like a virgin all over again.

Nobody would ever love me like this. And after that crap with Dad, Jack proved that he loved me more than my own family. More than the entire world.

I held him close, taking one more kiss before he slowly pulled way. He laid next to me, bracing me against his chest. We stared at each other for a long time.

Just being with him was a pleasure. He made naked and lazy a guilty thrill.

"Have you gotten everything?" I asked.

"Oh, yeah. Best part is we're just getting started. We're gonna do it over and over again, baby, 'til I know the job is done." He kissed me.

I smiled beneath his lips, knowing it wouldn't be long at all before he was ready for another round.

"Yeah? What about after I'm pregnant?"

"Then I'll make sure I find a place that's better than this club room. We need a real home outside the MC, just like the older guys with families." He laughed a little and shrugged, staring at the ceiling, full of new dreams.

" It's fucking insane. Never thought I'd be hatching plans like that. Not this soon, anyway."

He reached for my hand. Twining his fingers with mine, he pulled me closer on his chest.

"No, that's great, but it isn't what I meant…will you still want me when I'm not so small anymore?"

Jack's head jerked to face me. He stared for a second, wide-eyed disbelief written everywhere.

"You kidding? You're gonna be beautiful to me forever, Rach. I don't get rid of things I love. Had the same Harley since I was patched in by Pop ten years ago. You're my old lady, and I'll love you even when you really are an *old lady.*"

I laughed at his emphasis on the words.

"It's not funny, and it isn't bullshit either," he insisted. "Do I need to remind you? What does it say right here?"

He took my arm and held it up to my face. There in the slight red halo around the ink, I saw the words again, as if from a dream.

Property of Throttle, Prairie Devils Cassandra.

"Like it or not, you're mine," he growled, squeezing my flesh in that possessive way that sent lightning through my nerves.

"Oh, I like it," I said. I moved in for another kiss, reaching for the erection I felt rising against my thigh.

"Good. Because once something's mine, I never let up. Give me a couple years and you'll get all the house, jewelry, and kids you can handle."

I laughed, amazed at the image. It was so real I could see it.

"As long as I'm above ground, you're my old lady. Nobody and nothing's ever gonna change that." Jack stopped to kiss away the silly tear that trickled down my cheek. "We've had our fill with words. Let's get back to working on that baby…"

Smiling, I spread myself wide to receive him, ready for our forever.

Never again would I deny the badass I was spending the rest of my life with.

Thanks!

Want more Nicole Snow? Sign up for my newsletter to hear about new releases, subscriber only goodies, and other fun stuff!

JOIN THE NICOLE SNOW NEWSLETTER! - http://eepurl.com/HwFW1

Thank you so much for buying this ebook. I hope my romances will brighten your mornings and darken your evenings with total pleasure. Sensuality makes everything more vivid, doesn't it?

If you liked this book, please consider leaving a review and checking out my other erotic romance tales.

Got a comment on my work? Email me at nicolesnowerotica@gmail.com. I love hearing from my fans!

Kisses,
Nicole Snow

More Erotic Romance by Nicole Snow

KEPT WOMEN: TWO FERTILE SUBMISSIVE STORIES

SUBMISSIVE'S FOLLY (SEDUCED AND RAVAGED)

SUBMISSIVE'S EDUCATION

SUBMISSIVE'S HARD DISCOVERY

HER STRICT NEIGHBOR

SOLDIER'S STRICT ORDERS

COWBOY'S STRICT COMMANDS

FIGHT FOR HER HEART

BIG BAD DARE: TATTOOS AND SUBMISSION

SEXY SAMPLES: BIG BAD DARE

"Just you and I now," Garrett said.

He tipped the tumbler to his firm lips and knocked back his drink in one swig. I was only halfway done with mine, feeling it burning its way through my stomach and straight up to my brain.

"How about that dare?" He raised his eyebrows and slid in closer to me, wrapping his arm around my shoulder once more. "I didn't just bring you to this place to talk. How about some one on one time, Jessie? Doesn't the Princess underneath get tired of everyone treating her like a good girl?"

Yes!

"Sure," I mumbled, licking stray liquor from my bottom lip. "It does get really old. Hell, even I'm getting tired of it. Just one night, I'd like to be a little bad."

"Then you've come to the right man."

I laughed. Drunken revery set in, making my arms and legs move with evil confidence. I reached for his collar and pulled.

Garrett locked his hand around my wrist. He tugged me in, kicking the table back, pulling me onto his lap.

Then those huge hands were on my back, blazing up my flesh, searching for the zipper to my dress. He tugged me closer at the same time he unsheathed me, drawing me in for a kiss.

His lips stroked mine. And I thought the fruity alcohol had a bite! His kiss arced past my lips twice as fast, hot and sultry, streaming straight to the ends of my nerves.

Everything inside me opened at once. My legs, my lips, plowing apart to make way for his tongue, his hands.

Garrett saw his opportunity and seized it. Ruthlessly entitled, without a shred of doubt.

His free hand caught the ends of my hair and tugged. He locked my head in place, pushing his lips harder into mine, flicking his tongue into my mouth and rolling its wonderfully wet length back again.

Tease.

Or so I thought. His next kiss went much deeper, a full force imprint with tongue and teeth and strength.

I gurgled soft pleasure into his mouth. His tongue searched deep, seeking mine. When he found it, he held it down, sucking at my delicate lips, aiming his shocks through my flesh.

"What's the matter, Princess? Haven't you ever been kissed like that before?" He pulled back, staring into my sex starved eyes.

"It's been too long," I lied. I wasn't going to admit that he was the finest thing I'd ever had my hands and lips locked around.

"And here I wanted to introduce you to something new. Maybe I still can. Stand up…"

Look for Big Bad Dare online at your favorite retailer!

Hot Stories By My Friends!

Bear King's Curves by A.T. Mitchell

HIS CROWN. HIS CURVES. HIS FATED MATE.

Lyla Redd has just stolen her last precious artifact from the Klamath Bear Clan. The curvy smuggler got away with it before, but she doesn't know serious danger can arrive anytime in big, dark, and very muscular packages.

When werebear Alpha Nick Tunder lays eyes on the voluptuous beauty he's been sent to kill, he realizes the mission is a bust. Taking back his people's treasure is the easy part. Keeping Lyla away proves much harder, especially when she pursues and ends up in his bed for a thorough spanking.

Then the other Klamath bears find a human woman on their turf. Fur and claws fly as Lyla is sentenced to a darker fate.

Soaring passions hide much to explore, just like the mysterious artifact that brought them together. Deep love, lust, and an answer to their woes in an ancient royal bloodline are almost in reach, if only they can put the pieces together and their hearts on the line.

Destiny makes very strange bedfellows and beautiful fated mates…

This 38,000+ BBW shifter romance contains steam and language that'll make a grizzly roar. Batten down the hatches!

The Alpha's Touch – 14 Book Romance Boxed Set!

Deliciously dominant and wickedly possessive, alpha males are the ultimate lovers. Experience the dark passion of an alpha's touch in this exclusive box set of billionaires, shifters, rock stars, cops, outlaws, bounty hunters and more.

This special collection brings you 14 of the hottest alpha male romance stories ever told from the hottest New York Times, USA Today, Amazon and Barnes & Noble bestselling authors in the romance genre - all together in one amazing box set!

Look for these hot romance titles online at your favorite retailer!.

Printed in Great Britain
by Amazon